SCHOOL FOR NURSES

by

T. SAYERS ELLIS

Published by **CHIMERA**
ISBN 9781780807591

Nurse, Nurse

Suzanne worked at a hospital where the nurses' uniforms were a bit too short in the skirt for her taste, although her best friend, Marie, really looked good in hers. They had come up through nursing school together and found their first posting together - two years in the Geriatric Ward of Waterman Town Centre hospital.

Sue quickly settled into her new routine. Her life revolved around the ward with its cold blue tiles, coughing old men, the endless beeps and groans of the life-support machines, and sharing a small rented apartment with Marie. She was happy enough, but she felt something must be missing. And then, one morning, she had a shock.

She had just arrived home from her nightshift and was taking her tea when Marie dashed across their small kitchen, obviously late for her own shift. She was naked, and her lovely breasts were still wet from the shower. She was running a towel through her damp blonde curls, and shaking water off her body like some parody of an erotic dancer, in an effort to dry herself as quickly as possible.

'Can I borrow a uniform, Sue?' she asked, not seeming to notice the colour rushing into her roommate's cheeks. 'I'm dead if I don't get out of here in two minutes flat!'

Sue nodded, somewhat taken aback by the request, and lowered her eyes to her steaming mug of tea. Marie dashed off again down the short hall, a tuft of blonde hair peeking out below the tight white cheeks of her bottom between her slender thighs. Sue realised with horror that she could not stop staring at it until Marie disappeared into her room. She had honestly never thought about her friend in any way resembling... well, she had never thought of her *sexually*, even though she did enjoy shopping for clothes with her and helping her pick out the tightest outfits, the skimpiest lingerie and the smallest bathing tops...

'Must dash! You're an angel!' Marie breezed into the kitchen again, barely able to finish zipping Sue's slightly smaller uniform over her full, bra-free breasts. She gave her a quick peck on the cheek, and Sue found herself reaching up to touch her face in wonder as the door slammed closed behind her friend.

This will certainly not do, Sue thought sternly as she walked into hospital that night to begin a new shift. She had spent a restless day in bed tossing and turning, unable to sleep. She was pretty tired now and she had not even started work yet.

All day long, visions of Marie - Marie with her blonde curls peeping out from between the tops of her toned thighs; Marie with her firm, lovely breasts jewelled by water droplets; Marie's gorgeous face gazing at her anxiously as she dried her naked body off with a towel - haunted her and would not let her sleep in peace. She had found herself reaching down between her legs and feeling the wetness there, and then a delicious explosion would rock her body at the thought of sinking to her knees before the wetness Marie had been drying between her thighs, and burying her face in it...

She entered the Geriatric Unit. An old man was shuffling out of the cold Victorian toilet and returning slowly to his bed. A light had been left on at the nurses' desk. Usually there were more nurses around at the change of shift, and stepping behind the desk, Sue found a note that explained their absence. The staff was short tonight because two of the Sisters were out with the flu.

'Hi!'

Suzanne suddenly felt soft, familiar hands covering her eyes from behind.

'Marie,' she whispered.

'Got it in one!' Giggling, Marie moved around to face her. She was still wearing Sue's uniform, and it really was much too small for her. On Marie, the skirt - which even on Sue was too short - was a sexy mini, and the tightness of the bodice straining to contain her generous breasts made her look utterly voluptuous. Her appearance was completely improper for a professional nurse, especially since she had let the zipper down a little in front to relieve the pressure on her bosom, offering a teasing view of her luscious cleavage to anyone who cared to look.

'Guess who's been drafted to pull a double shift?' Marie made a disgruntled face for a half-hearted second before her usual smile returned. 'But guess who's also found us a nice little earner?'

Sue gazed at her with a puzzled expression.

Marie pulled her deeper into the recesses behind the Sister's desk as if to make sure no one in the dark ward could hear her. 'There's no one here tonight,' she whispered conspiratorially.

The accidental touch of her friend's soft, warm breasts against her arm made Sue shiver. 'That's right,' she acknowledged, unable to look Marie in the eye. It was embarrassing having her so close, and she was ashamed of her secret physical reaction. *Stop it*! she thought, admonishing her body, *stop it right now*!

'We've got a live one in private room seven,' Marie went on, oblivious to her friend's internal struggle.

'Mr Walker?' Sue welcomed the distraction. 'He's harmless enough, a nice old boy.'

'A nice old boy who offered me two-hundred pounds to strip for him!' Marie exclaimed beneath her breath.

'He did *what*?' Sue was stunned.

'I know,' Marie sounded equally shocked, but evidently for a different reason, 'the cheapskate! I got him to make it five-hundred for the two of us.' She smiled wickedly into her friend's eyes.

Sue was even more stunned. 'You got... but I... but I *can't*,' she gasped. 'You're crazy, Marie!'

'Not even for me?' Her roommate pouted even while fixing her with a challenging stare.

Sue's cheeks coloured in alarm, for she knew what was coming and she would have to struggle to resist the mental arm-twisting.

'Not even for your best friend, who desperately needs the money, and who let you move into her flat when you had nowhere else to go?'

That was unfair, but true nonetheless, and Sue found her resistance wilting as her breathing became shaky. 'Do we really have to?' she asked weakly.

'I *do* need the money,' Marie whispered seductively, and clearly sensing victory, she picked this perfect moment to stroke Sue's silky fringe away from her flushed brow. Their bodies were pressed up against each other's in the small alcove behind the desk, one set of curves gently moulding into another. 'You know I do, Sue,' she murmured. 'And besides, he's a bit of an old codger, but it might be fun.'

Sue swallowed hard and closed her eyes so Marie would not see her thoughts as she nodded reluctantly.

Mr Walker's room was filled with shadows; only a single lamp was lit by the elderly man's bed where he lay snoring lightly. Marie crept into the room first, and then waved Sue in after glancing quickly up and down the corridor to make sure no one else was about. They could all die up and down the ward for the next half hour, Sue thought, yet strangely enough, she could not find it in herself to feel guilty about her frivolously unprofessional attitude. She was far too excited about being with Marie as she followed the sexy, shapely form of her friend into the quiet room.

Although Sue had never been consciously attracted to another female before, Marie looked absolutely mouth-watering to her now as she bent over the old man's bed. Mr Walker stirred, and his snoring came to an abrupt halt as his eyes squinted open, and caught sight of Marie's half unzipped dress looming over his face.

'If you've got the money now, Mr Walker,' she leaned in closer to him as she spoke softly, 'I believe you have a private show to enjoy.'

With her help the man struggled up into a sitting position, and supported by numerous pillows, he counted out a small pile of notes onto the mobile table used for meals and wheeled into place beside him by the nurses. Ten crisp fifty-pound notes now lay on the table. Marie made to pick them up, but the old man's hand moved with surprising swiftness to slap her arm away. 'Not before the curtain falls,' he said. 'I want to see the warm-up act first.' He looked directly at Sue, and she realised with a small shock that she would have to undress in front of both of them to get things rolling.

'You didn't say I'd have to do this cold,' she complained beneath her breath to Marie when her friend walked encouragingly up beside her.

'Keep him sweet,' Marie whispered, 'we could get more out of him if we do this right.' She glanced back at the old man wearing her sexiest smile.

Mr Walker's wallet was under his pillow again, but it was by no means empty. He sat up a little higher, his yellow hands clutching the sheet over his chest, and gazed lecherously at Sue's shapely bottom as she turned away coyly before slowly pulling her crisp uniform up over her head without unzipping it. Then she stood waiting, her back still to him, wondering what on earth she was doing

4

standing there only in her white bra, white stockings and suspenders, and small white panties.

'Come here, my dear girl,' the old man said in a dry, raspy voice.

Her belly churning, she turned to face both patient and nurse, and she blushed as much from the feel of Marie's eyes on her body as from the old man's stare as he crooked a finger to beckon her closer.

Anxiously glancing at Marie, Sue found herself obeying him until she stood beside her friend again. Her thighs brushed the edge of the bed close beside him, easily within his reach should he want to touch her, but all he did was point at her panties. She blushed even more deeply, understanding his silent demand.

Marie nodded once, encouraging her to carry on, and Sue was stunned to see a fierce light burning in her friend's eyes. She looked away quickly, yet she found herself obeying the sensuous nurse as she eased her panties down, and shivered to feel the cool air of the quiet room kiss her bare bottom... and worse, it made her shamefully conscious of the wetness between her thighs as she slipped the fine cotton all the way down her legs to the floor. She stepped out of them daintily, and that left only her bra, stockings and suspenders.

The old man's eyes devoured the nubile vision before him. 'Now you help your friend,' he instructed.

Still blushing furiously, Sue found herself reaching for Marie.

When they had both lost their uniforms, Sue could not help but wonder at how beautiful her friend was, and at her nearly uncontrollable desire to kiss and suck her large breasts. She wanted to sink to her knees before Marie right then and there and bury her face in the tight wet curls of her intoxicatingly fragrant pubic hair... she gasped, distracted from her fantasy when she suddenly felt one of the old man's hands on her bare buttocks.

Marie said firmly, 'No touching, unless you want to pay more.'

Negotiations ensued, but the old man's hand remained possessively on Sue's bottom for the duration. Finally he and Marie had agreed on the terms and Sue felt his clammy, possessive touch slip away. She realised then that she should have been listening. Apparently, the touching to be allowed was not to be done by Mr Walker. She saw his wallet appear from beneath the pillow again, and ten more notes were counted out on the table, only to disappear into Marie's discarded uniform.

Strangely dazed, Sue heard words floating in the air before her, but for some bizarre reason she could not string them together to make any sense. She heard her name mentioned, but she could not seem to concentrate on the dialogue and what it meant. It was as though the whole scene was turning into a dream in which she was completely powerless to do anything while her behaviour was manipulated for pleasure and profit.

She watched Marie elegantly perch herself on the edge of the wooden table over the old man's bed, and spread her legs. Her friend then beckoned to her without a word, and Sue found herself climbing up over Mr Walker's blankets, her knees on either side of him so her bare bottom was presented directly before his appreciative face. She was between Marie's gloriously parted thighs, looking up into her gorgeous friend's hypnotic eyes.

'Kiss me,' Marie whispered with a hint of triumphant mischief. 'It's all for a good cause.'

Sue's head sank willingly into the heady scent of Marie's blonde curls, her mouth hanging open in breathless gratitude.

Marie's head rolled back, and she groaned deep in her throat, inhaling sharply as Sue's first tentative kisses became more confident and her tongue found its way deep into her hot, wet furrow. She licked softly and insistently until her friend came on the small table with a shudder that made her breasts quiver.

Marie quickly recovered herself, however, and giggled as the old man's wallet once again emerged from behind the pillows. 'Don't move,' she instructed in a firm but friendly voice, and utterly dazed now, Sue held her position, Marie's wetness shining on her cheeks, her naked bottom still presented to the old man's face. She did not truly comprehend what he said; she heard only his wheezy snigger and the soft rustling of money being counted again. And then Marie slipped down from her perch and whispered, 'Hold on, darling, it won't take him long.'

'Take him long for what?' Sue gasped, but Marie simply moved the table away, guided her a little further down the bed, and then held firmly on to her wrists. Sue looked helplessly up into her flatmate's eyes. 'What do you want me to do now?' she asked softly.

'Just hold still,' Marie replied, and leaned over to kiss her lips. It was a gentle kiss, a lovely kiss, so soft and affectionate that Sue became wonderfully lost in it, only realising as it went on that it was distracting her from what was happening behind her...

The old man's leathery and bony hand was touching her bottom again. She felt it move away, there was a pause during which she held her breath and closed her eyes, and then he spanked her naked cheeks. She gasped in pain, because his hand was as tough as a wicker carpet beater.

'You naughty young thing!' He wheezed, and spanked her again with amazing strength.

'Mm!' she tried to protest, but Marie's kiss was too insistent, her tongue darting around hers and weakening her resistance.

'You naughty, naughty thing!' the old man repeated sternly. 'How dare you wake me up and then do what you just did with your friend, right in front of me, on my bed? I'm going to give you the spanking your behaviour deserves!'

Never before had Sue been spanked, nor had she ever considered being spanked, but the hand of Mr Walker kept rising and falling and making her bottom so painfully hot she was very grateful when this unjust punishment finally ceased. But then she nearly jumped out of her skin when she felt his gristly body pressing up against hers. It was obvious his pyjama trousers were undone, gaping open to expose his crotch, and she tried to look back over her shoulder to see what he was up to, but Marie would not let her.

'Keep still, my darling,' she murmured into Sue's ear, and pressed her friend's flushed face between her cushiony breasts.

Sue gasped against the warm, enveloping flesh as she felt Mr Walker's erect penis probing between her thighs, nudging its way closer to her exposed pussy. And then, unbelievably, she felt his rigid old cock slip between the wet lips of her sex, and penetrate her. Soft warm hands cupped and caressed her dazed face as leathery cold hands cupped and squeezed her buttocks. Then Marie's tongue invaded her mouth again in a passionate kiss and Sue came, impaled on the old man's gnarled rod, just as his cool and ancient seed erupted deep inside her warm young flesh.

Sins

It is a little room, almost nothing more than a cubicle, surprisingly small for a headmaster's office. It contains the desk behind which he is seated, and a chair for me, with nothing to hide behind. His hair is going stylishly grey at his temples to match his eyes. 'Sit down,' he instructs. 'I'll just look this over.' He extracts a file from one of his desk drawers, a creamy manila folder from which the tips of pink slips stick out like mischievous little tongues. He opens the folder as I seat myself, crossing my arms over my chest to hold my raincoat closed. 'Don't sit with your raincoat on,' he says without looking up again.

I promptly get up to take it off.

'Did I tell you to stand?' he asks softly, still studying the pink slips by the light of a small desk lamp with a flexible steel neck. It is the only light in the room; there are no windows.

'I thought...'

'You don't know how to think,' he points out firmly, 'that's why you're here. Sit down. If you knew how to think, or even just how to add up a simple column of figures, you wouldn't be here.'

Still wearing my raincoat, I resume my seat feeling foolish and confused. My stomach churns as I smooth down my cotton skirt. Normally I don't wear skirts, but in small print on the back of the summons was written wear a *skirt to the punishment*.

'You have your voucher?'

I pull it out of my right pocket, a ticket stub like the kind you get at the movies, only it was the guard downstairs at the iron arch who gave me this. I lean forward to hand it to him, but then place it awkwardly on the desk beside the folder when he makes no move to accept it.

'Your statement.' It is not a question; it is a command given an impatient edge by what almost sounds like boredom.

I turn in the chair, and pull one of the pocket's of my raincoat inside-out in my haste to extract a yellow slip of paper. I quickly place it on the desk just inside the circle of light, nervously smoothing its crumpled edges for him.

'Don't fuss,' he snaps.

I snatch my hand back as though scalded by his cold voice.

He leans back in his chair, slips a cigarette out of a pack lying just outside the halo of light, and brings it to life with the hot blue flame of a silver lighter. Smoke streams out from between his lips as he asks, 'Cigarette?'

I swallow nervously, and shake my head.

'Oh, go on...' he urges mildly, 'go on...'

I smile weakly.

'You know you want to,' he adds, staring into my eyes.

I lean forward, and reach tentatively for the pack.

He slaps my hand back. 'Bad girl. Two more demerits.' He picks up a pen with his free hand and makes a note in my file.

I gasp, 'But you...'

'"Lead us not into temptation",' he quotes without looking up. 'It's your job to make sure you don't get led astray. I can't always be there looking out for you.'

I glance around the room. I don't see any paddles, or any other instruments of correction, and I wonder what he is going to punish me with.

Dropping the pen, he deliberately knocks some ash onto the floor. 'Pick that up for me,' he says.

My eyebrows arch questioningly.

'Pick that up for me,' he repeats. 'Are you deaf?'

I get up, walk around the desk, and then sink down onto my hands and knees to scoop some of the ashes up onto my fingertips.

'Use this.' He hands me the statement of my demerits.

I run the edge of the paper beneath the ashes, and flick them into the wastebasket beside the desk.

'Good,' he says, 'very good. Now take off your coat.'

My knees feel weak as I stand up and the blood rushes to my head. He is so close, only a hand's length away. I start unbuttoning my raincoat.

He follows my fingers with his eyes, moving down from one button to another as he raises the cigarette to his lips, and lowers it again, blowing the smoke away from me so as not to obscure his view. He is staring at my breasts, which are visible now between the flaps of my coat, and I feel myself blushing. I am standing before him in a short skirt, flat shoes, gym socks and nothing else, all according to the warrant, which clearly states, *no shirt and no panties, nothing between skin and the outer shell at punishment.*

'Go on,' he says patiently.

I turn around slowly, feeling his eyes on my bare skin as I shrug the stiff material off my shoulders. The cool air caresses my back where I've been perspiring between my shoulder blades against the silk lining. My skirt rides up slightly beneath a gentle electric current of static-cling as I slip the coat off completely, and take a few steps away from the desk to hang it on a hook behind the door.

'Now turn around.'

I fight the urge to cross my arms over my naked breasts as I turn to face him again.

'Put your hands behind your back.'

Standing perfectly still, I obey him, staring at his face while he studies my breasts.

'Eyes straight ahead,' he commands.

I reluctantly look away from his intent expression.

'Shoulders square and legs at ease,' he elaborates tersely.

I pull my shoulders back, and feel my soft mounds thrust up and out as I do so. My nipples are already hard from the prolonged weight of his eyes.

'Good,' he says approvingly. 'Now, come here.'

I focus on him again as he puts his cigarette out in a glass ashtray, casually crushing the butt beneath his thumb.

'Come sit right here where I can look at you.' He pushes his chair back.

There is no mistaking where he means, and I am surprised by my own lack of hesitation as I go and perch on the edge of the desk in front of him.

'Sit on it.'

I lift my bum carefully up onto the hard surface, but I cannot keep from rustling some papers in the process, and then shyly cross my arms over my bare breasts again.

'Hands on your head,' he says sternly, 'and don't crease the statements you're sitting on or that'll be more demerits added to your tab.'

I raise my arms and plant my hands on my head. I am squeezed between him and the edge of the desk, my skirt almost brushing his black trousers.

He looks up at my face and then down at my lap, and I spread my thighs apart so his legs can come forward under the desk and close the gap between us without touching. I am sitting on a man's desk in a very small room, naked except for a skirt that ends just above my knees, with my legs spread wide.

'Let me just make sure you understand.' He leans forward so I feel his breath on my skin as he speaks. 'The system mandates that charges incurred and not met require that each separate erogenous zone be punished in increasingly intimate steps according to the scale of the debt. Because you have acquired so many debits,' he glances briefly down at the pink statements lying between my thighs, 'you are obliged to come bare-breasted and wearing nothing beneath your skirt. Am I right?'

I nod, feeling light-headed.

'So, with this many demerits outstanding, I get to do this...' He reaches up and grabs my left nipple between his thumb and forefinger. 'I get to massage it, and press it...'

I gasp as he pinches my nipple.

'I get to pull it...' He tugs on it gently, and I find myself bending forward towards his mouth as his other hand comes up to touch my right breast. I recoil, because for some reason I am not ready for this yet, but he grasps my whole breast firmly, holding my body in place as his mouth reaches my left nipple. Still gripping it between his fingers, he tongues the very tip of it.

'Oh!' I cry softly.

He takes his hand off my right breast as my body leans willingly into his mouth, and his tongue orbits my tense nipple for a few more seconds before he

9

suddenly sits back.

'I can also explore your oral reflexes.' His right hand caresses the side of my neck on its way up, and his fingers lightly stroke my cheek before he presses his thumb against my mouth.

Moaning stubbornly, I keep my lips sealed.

Very gently, he bites my nipple.

'Oh!' I exclaim again, and his thumb slips into my mouth. I close my eyes and suck on it blindly, not understanding my reaction but not really questioning it either.

'Good girl,' he murmurs, and we sit there with his mouth working on my firm nipple and my tongue working on his hard thumb until he suddenly pulls it out and pushes his chair back. My nipple immediately feels cold without his warm lips around it, bereft, and I shiver to feel the room's chilly air on my chest again.

'I think you're ready now,' he says. 'How many demerits was it?'

I lift my thigh slightly so he can pull the statement out from beneath it.

'Ah, *this* many. Would you prefer having your skirt on, or off?'

'Do I...?'

'Do you have a choice? No, of course not. I am only offering you a courtesy, as a gentleman. Would you like to have a cigarette and think about it?'

I look at him anxiously.

'You've already got two demerits for it, you can't get more, so why not enjoy the smoke? Go on,' he holds the pack up for me, 'you know you want to.'

I take the cigarette from the packet, and he lights it for me. His silver lighter flashes in the lamplight as he snaps it closed, and I take my first puff. The room feels funny as the smoke fills my lungs.

'Very good.' He smiles as I exhale. 'You understand your debts were sufficient to necessitate the punishment of both your mouth and your breasts, but now, of course...' He leans back in his chair. 'Another four on the bill, plus expenses. I don't smoke. You'll have to cover the cost of the cigarettes, I'm afraid; they're your little weakness. That gives me your bottom for punishment, and... oh, I suppose that gives me everything. Lift your skirt. Don't make me wait.'

'But I didn't *want* the cigarette,' I protest breathlessly.

'I only bought the pack because I knew you'd want one,' he corrects me, and puts one of his hands on my thigh beneath the skirt. 'Never mind, just take your time. Finish the cigarette.' Slowly, he slides his hand up to my bottom, and then lifting it slightly brings it back down again hard.

'Oh!' I exclaim.

'Get up and bend over the desk,' he orders in a thick voice.

I glance down at the hard-on straining against his slacks as my feet touch the floor and I turn around obediently. I feel his eyes on my bottom, and then his hands as he parts my warm cheeks.

'This won't take long,' he whispers in my ear before he spanks me again.

His skin stings mine as it strikes and how hard his palm is comes as a shock that spreads a strangely delicious heat through my body. He spanks me again, and then again, and I feel my face getting as red as my bum from the shame of realising I am enjoying this.

'It won't take long at all,' he assures me softly, 'but first, a little something just for you, so you won't think I'm here only for my own pleasure.'

I glance over my shoulder at him when I hear the sound of his zipper coming down, but then quickly look away again as his cock springs free and I feel him spread my cheeks open.

'Good thing you girls don't smoke cigars,' he remarks as he pushes his rigid penis into my tight bottom. I arch my back, helping his painfully rampant erection sink deep into my clinging, perversely welcoming, flesh. 'With the cost of tobacco these days...' he groans as he thrusts hard into my body's most private and sensitive parts, 'you'd be tied up in here all day!'

I reach down to caress my button, and as he pumps his hot come into my burning sphincter I climax with him, biting my lip not to scream from the terrible pleasure.

And then he makes me lick his cock clean before he lights another cigarette.

Parking Lot Spanking

My husband often makes me take down my panties in public. The first time it happened was at the supermarket. I have a D-cup figure with shapely hips, and I never have problems getting men to look at me, but what happened this time was different.

I had left George waiting in the car and gone back to the counter to buy a pack of gum after we finished our weekly shopping. As was my habit in the past, I got lost reading a magazine by the checkout and didn't notice the time flying by. When I eventually bought my gum and got back to the car, George was redder than a bull's eye and twice as hot under the collar.

'You've done this too many times, Darlene,' he said as I slipped into the passenger's seat.

'What are you talking about?' I asked innocently.

'You know what I'm talking about, Darlene.'

He was real mad this time, I could tell; there was a little white vein over his right eye that was twitching. It was boiling hot in the parking lot in the noonday sun, and people were walking by. 'I don't know what you're talking about, George.' I continued my innocent act. 'Start the car and turn on the air-conditioner, please,' I added casually, hoping he would let me get away with it.

He did not. George is a big man with sandy hair thinning on top. He has freckles on his arms, big red freckles on big strong arms. I like him to love me hard, usually he's too gentle, but this time he really lost his temper. Without another word, he grabbed my wrist and dragged me across the seat toward him. Then he opened his door, got out the car, and pulled me with him.

I was suddenly very scared of this man I thought I knew as I stood in the hot parking lot, my short skirt wafting against the backs of my thighs in the breeze, trying to think of what I could say to calm him down. 'George, honey...'

'Don't say a word Darlene, just walk around to the back of the car.'

'George...'

'Darlene, if you say another word, I'm going to drive off and you can walk home.'

He meant it. I could see it in the set of his mouth and in the slight sheen of perspiration on his upper lip. 'All right,' I said as quietly as possible, and walked around to the back of the car. We own an old, four-door Ford with a big boot. I stood next to it, and the hot bumper made me jump slightly when it touched my naked legs beneath my skirt.

'Darlene,' George came and stood right in front of me, so his face was looming over mine, 'you've been a naughty, naughty girl. Wouldn't you say?'

'I would, George,' I admitted quietly.

'Then you ought to be punished, right?'

'Um...' I wasn't quite sure what was happening.

'Push your panties down and lean over the back of the car, Darlene.'

I couldn't believe it. My ears rang with his shocking command as I blushed just thinking about it. And yet, at the same time, the idea made my pussy feel strangely warm. 'George, come on now, honey...'

'Darlene...'

'I'm not going to take my panties down like some kind of tramp and bend over the car,' I protested.

'Darlene, you want to stay here? Fine, I'm done with you.' He started walking back down the driver's side.

'George?!'

He turned back towards me. 'Get your face on that boot, Darlene.'

'But it's shameful... I mean, out here in public...'

'You should have thought about what it would feel like to take your panties down in the parking lot before you kept me waiting.'

'I didn't know...'

'You will now.'

Which is how I found myself bending over that boot in broad daylight in the parking lot of the busiest supermarket in town. Luckily, we had parked near a corner where the traffic wasn't too heavy. But I could still hear people walking by even though I couldn't see them, and didn't *want* to see them.

'That's a good girl, Darlene.' I heard George come and stand behind me. 'Very good.'

I felt his hands reach up under my skirt and stroke my thighs from behind. I felt the air on my skin as my skirt was lifted, exposing my little white cotton panties, and I suddenly felt faint knowing my bottom was now exposed to the eyes of any man or woman who happened to pass by. I closed my own eyes. 'George...' I whispered.

'Be a very good girl, Darlene.' He peeled the soft cotton off my buttocks and slowly pulled my panties down. His strong hands caressed me on the way down, and the breeze kissing my pussy made me realise I was wet; I was horribly embarrassed and yet excited at the same time. He took his time sliding my panties down my thighs, so I had plenty of time to think about what I was letting him do in the middle of a crowded parking lot, and then he left them hanging around my knees.

'George?' I sounded like a frightened little girl now, yet the hot feeling between my legs was not at all innocent.

'Hold still, honey,' he said, and right then and there he started spanking me. The impact of his open palm stung like the slap of water when you dive flat into a pool, and sent ripples of pleasure through my soaking pussy. Suddenly I wanted him badly. He slapped my left cheek first, and then my right cheek, and I gasped in mingled pain and desire. He brought his hand down hard on my exposed flesh six times before he patted my flaming bottom, and told me to scoot back into the car.

He drove us home like a criminal running from the cops, and shoved me into the bedroom the minute we walked into the house. 'You know what to do,' he said in a low voice, the same one he had used in the parking lot.

'You want me to take everything off?' I teased.

'If you want, we can go back to the parking lot,' he said roughly, 'and this time we can park right outside the checkout aisles.'

I took my panties off but left my skirt on, and then pulled off my T-shirt. I wasn't wearing a bra.

He grabbed both my breasts and squeezed them roughly, as hungrily as if I was a girl he had never had before and he had finally got me in the backseat of a car.

I sighed, 'George, honey, love me like your own little bad girl!'

He pulled my skirt up and made me kneel on the edge of the bed with my bum up in the air. I didn't know what he was doing, but then I heard a strange hissing sound and looked around. He was pulling his belt off one loop at a time, letting it hang down his leg as he held it up by the buckle. He patted my bottom just beneath my cheeks, making my pussy tremble, and then stepped back.

The first lash of the belt was the worst; it was such a shock to my system. The belt flicked around and stung both my cheeks, but not at the same time, so it almost felt like two blows right after the other. I started crying after his third hard lash, but I knew better than to complain.

He kept on touching my cheeks in between whipping them, making me so wet that I finally collapsed across the bed and buried my face in a pillow I wanted him so badly.

He was kissing me now, and the feel of his hand between my thighs made me moan with longing. Then I finally sensed him pulling his cock out of his pants. He rolled me over onto my back, and made me lift my legs up into the air and hold them wide open for him. I felt totally exposed as he slowly fed my hungry pussy his huge red cock. I had never seen it get so big before, and I cried out as he drove it into me.

'Are you a bad girl?' he asked harshly, fucking me hard and fast.

'I want to be good!' I gasped. He was filling me up, violently stuffing me with his erection like he never had before, and I wanted to die it felt so good.

'Will you take your punishment like a good girl?' he demanded, making my breasts bob wildly up and down as he rammed his hard-on as deep into my body as he could.

'I will honey, I will! I'll be just as bad as you want me to be! I'll be your good... oh, I'll be your punishment whore!' I screamed.

He leaned over and bit my neck as I came and came and came. Sometimes being bad is the best thing that can happen to a girl.

Going Down to the Movies

Not much was happening on the home front for a while until I came home one night last year, and found a note from Mark on the kitchen table. Mark is a movie buff. When we first met we went out to the movies constantly, especially to sexy Italian flicks from the sixties. But lately, what with one thing or another - you know how it is once you start living together - even racy European movies had stopped getting us excited. Then one night I came home and found a note on the kitchen table in Mark's handwriting: *We're going to the movies. Go to the bedroom.*

Intrigued, I took off my coat. Beneath it I was wearing a cotton blouse and a wool skirt. I went into the bedroom hoping to find him. Instead, on the closet door near the bed, was another note: *Take out your raincoat.*

I took my raincoat out of the closet. It was tan vinyl with a red lining and I'd had it for years. Pinned to the neck of the coat was another note: *Put it on, with nothing between you and the buttons.*

My pussy started getting wet right then and there; it had been tingling since I walked through the bedroom door. Mystery games had thrilled me since I was a kid, and Mark knew it. I stripped off my blouse, and got butterflies in my stomach looking around our little apartment wondering if Mark was hiding somewhere, watching me. We had been living together for six months, yet I suddenly felt shy. I let my skirt drop to the floor, undid the clasp on my bra, slipped it off, and folded it neatly on a pillow. Then I slid my panties down to my ankles, stepped out of them and picked up the raincoat. The red lining skidded against my already tight and excited nipples as I slipped it on, and the plastic chafed my bare thighs. The vinyl was cold and felt very strange against my naked breasts and buttocks.

Inside the left hip pocket, I found another note: *Go to the multi-screen theatre. Don't drive.*

Not far from our apartment there is a precinct with a big movie house in it, the kind with five screens and wide, comfortable seats. The thought of walking through the streets with no clothes on beneath the raincoat made my pussy tingle, but my belly felt tight with fear. Thinking fast, I decided that if Mark took the trouble to liven things up around here, the least I could do was swallow my inhibitions and play along.

I walked out into the hallway of our apartment building, and immediately felt a draft slip up into the coat and caress my thighs. I looked both ways to make sure no one was around, but it wasn't until I was out on the street that I really began feeling self-conscious. Every one I passed seemed to be looking at me in my raincoat and high-heels. My legs felt strangely weak, and I was increasingly worried about tripping and wantonly exposing my bare cheeks to the world as I fell. I kept my eyes lowered and stepped demurely away from all the men I passed. The two blocks between our apartment and the theatre had never seemed longer.

Inside the theatre I held the collar of the raincoat tightly closed, but at the ticket desk I suffered my next thrill of embarrassment. A young man handed me a stub through the window before I even opened my mouth, and when I looked at him in surprise, he said, 'You were expected,' and smiled at me in a way that made me feel he could see right through my coat. I blushed to realise that in my excitement I had forgotten to bring any money, and that until that moment I had not even thought about the actual movie.

I hurried down the appropriate corridor; I did not know if the film had started yet. I was glad to see the lobby was empty, but also a little disappointed; subconsciously, I had been looking forward to walking through a crowd of people completely naked beneath my coat.

I opened the door to the auditorium, stepped inside, and paused to let my eyes adjust to the darkness. Already I could tell the theatre was full, and gradually, with a sinking feeling in my belly, I realised the audience consisted mainly of men. All I remember about the movie when I came in is a woman's legs filling the screen and that it had been shot somewhere very bright. Then I noticed a section of five empty seats about halfway down the aisle, and somehow I knew Mark had managed to reserve them. But I would have to make my way over the legs of approximately ten seated men to get to them, and their knees pulling on my coat would threaten to expose me every step of the way.

I took a deep breath, and almost turned to walk out. Then a head looked back at me from directly behind the row of empty seats, and my heart leapt. It had to be Mark.

I made my way towards him while very firmly telling myself no one could possibly know I was naked beneath my coat. And yet... I swear one man touched my bottom through my coat when I said 'Excuse me' as I squeezed past him on my way to the empty seats, and once my coat parted so the light from the screen fell right on my bare pussy, but I'm pretty sure no one saw that.

I reached the empty seats, but I couldn't see Mark anywhere. Some guy told me to hurry up and sit down and I promptly obeyed, perspiring slightly with anxiety. I could not believe I was sitting nearly naked in a movie theatre full of men who were all probably sexually aroused by the action on the screen.

'Don't turn around,' a voice said softly from just behind me.

'Mark?' I whispered uncertainly, because I couldn't really be sure it was him.

'Shut it!' the voice hissed, 'or I'll tell everybody what a slut you are.'

A submissive thrill stabbed me straight between the legs. I could not be sure this man was Mark, and having a faceless voice talking to me like this as I sat naked beneath my thin coat in a dark room full of men was making my pussy melt.

'Spread your legs,' he commanded.

I took a deep breath, and parted my thighs.

'Now touch yourself.'

'What?' I whispered.

'You heard me.'

I had always felt awkward talking about masturbation with a man, not to mention doing it in front of him, let alone in front of several dozen men in a public place. I hesitated.

'Do it,' the voice insisted. 'Stick your finger in your pussy.'

I didn't turn around because I didn't want to; these firm commands from an anonymous source were seriously arousing me. With my trembling left hand I slowly lifted the left side of my coat off my thigh. Then, with my equally unsteady right hand, I parted the other side of my coat. Air wafted across my bare legs and felt wonderfully cool against my warm skin, but it felt especially good against my pussy, which was already so wet its juices were dampening the coat's red lining. I reached down and slipped a finger past the puffy lips of my labia. My clit was standing almost painfully at attention, all I had to do was circle it with my long fingernail to experience a stab of pleasure that made me suck my breath in.

'Get hot, baby.'

No one else seemed to hear the quietly demanding voice, and none of the men sitting in the row on either side of me seemed to notice me. Feeling a little bolder, I flicked my clit with my nail, and gasped.

'Hotter!' the voice said impatiently.

I played my index finger over my knob, pressing down on it firmly, and then ran it between the hot, swollen lips of my pussy. My breathing became fast and shallow, and yet still the voice said, 'More' and then 'More' again, until I was almost coming. I was nearly over the edge when a hand squeezed my shoulder. 'Now stop.'

'Mark?' I asked weakly.

'Close your eyes.'

I obeyed. I still had not turned around to see who the voice belonged to I was so into this little game of domination and submission. I sat tense with anticipation as I felt him climbing over the chair next to mine, and settling himself into it.

'Hold still,' he said.

I was so hot waiting for him to dictate the next step in our game that the soft sound of his slacks brushing the seat as he shifted his position seemed louder than the movie to me.

'Allow me.' He slipped three fingers up inside me so swiftly that I nearly cried out it felt so good. I sat up straight and grasped the armrests to brace myself.

16

'You like that, baby?'

I nodded, unable to speak as he began massaging my clitoris with the base of his palm, going around and around it while his other hand reached up to touch my neck and caress my face. His fingers moving steadily in and out of me made me buck in my seat as I rode the beginnings of what promised to be an intense orgasm. All I had to do to sharpen the edge of my pleasure was think about the fact that I was surrounded by men and completely naked beneath my coat while a man whose face I couldn't see put his hand up my throbbing pussy.

When he suddenly pressed his thumb against my lips and slipped it between them, I started coming in earnest. I took his thumb deep into my mouth, letting him dominate my throat, and climaxed like I never had before in my life. His hand gagging me stopped me from crying out, but I rocked back and slid forward in the seat and thrust my hips up around his fingers, grinding my clit against his hard palm.

After my orgasm finally stopped, he emptied my mouth, pulled on the belt around my waist so my coat fell open all the way, and yanked it off my shoulders. Cool air flowed over my perspiring skin while I kept my eyes closed, a wanton smile spreading across my face.

Still filling my pussy with one hand, he placed the other one on the back of my neck and began pushing me down. The coat stayed behind in the chair as my arms slipped out of it, and I felt his hand travel down my slick back as I crouched on my knees in a crowded hall and took the biggest cock I can ever remember so deep into my mouth that its head nudged the back of my throat.

I swallowed him whole, and then pulled back and sucked on his head for a moment before pushing my face down over him again. I felt him leaning forward, but I could not believe it when his hand smacked my bottom.

I froze.

Surely everyone had heard that! He spanked me again, and the low, flat sound was muffled by the soundtrack, but the sensation was not; it stung like buggery! I was getting spanked, naked, in front of countless unknown men! He kept punishing me slowly, one cheek at a time as I sucked hungrily on his dick.

Finally he stopped to grip my hot bottom, and I felt as though he was branding the marks of his fingers into my cheeks he squeezed them so viciously. I felt more than naked; I felt profoundly exposed in a way I never would have dreamed of letting myself be. Mark had never even mentioned spanking to me, and the hard, methodical blows made the aching need in my pussy deeper still.

Then I felt his erection jump and tighten in my mouth, and his cum started flooding down my throat. I swallowed mouthful after mouthful of his bittersweet milk, and yet there was so much of it that some seeped out from between my stretched lips to wet my cheeks and chin and throat. I felt deliciously drenched in his spunk by the time his cock slipped out of my mouth.

'You're such a quiet date to take to the late show,' he whispered.

I reached blindly for his hand, and kissed it.

We still go to the movies together, but now I wear a brand new leather coat he bought me as a wedding present.

Mandy

Amanda Vanforth rose out of her jasmine scented bathwater, trailing suds in her bare feet on the plush rug, and gazed at herself in the mirror. She was amply graced with firm, thirty-eight-D breasts whose nipples stiffened at the slightest naughty thought, a tight but still generous bottom, and a glorious fiery spray of red pubic hair to match the wet curls flowing down her back. Smiling, she dried herself off, sprayed perfume on her throat and breasts, and then chose a small, revealing striped top along with a pair of slacks that showed off her voluptuous hips. She was going to see Albert, her husband's brother, and Albert liked to admire her shapely buttocks.

She had always been able to manipulate Albert's interest in her to her own ends. This week, with Sidney out of town on business, she planned on coaxing Albert into buying more stock for her private portfolio with the company money, and the fact that he had asked to see her in his office gave her the perfect opportunity to do so. She did not plan on being married to Sidney forever, and when the time came, she intended to bail on him with a nice golden parachute.

Amanda walked into the last suite on the top floor and sauntered past the secretaries straight into Albert's office. The grey-headed old harpy who sat by his door rose when she appeared, but then sat down again as Amanda ignored her and pushed open the mahogany door leading into the light-filled space of her brother-in-law's office.

Only then did she stop short, because he was not sitting at his desk as he normally was, or even standing by one of the many windows.

'Albert?' she called. No one answered, but she felt the door close silently behind her, and turned quickly on her heels.

Albert was standing in the corner smoking a cigarette and watching her. This was not like him; he was usually hard at work behind his desk, and would spring up like a puppy to greet her when she entered. 'Hello Amanda,' he said, 'I've been expecting you.'

'Really? You've a funny way of showing it.'

He smiled. 'I have some things to show *you*.'

'Really?' she repeated, making an effort to sound interested. He often tried to impress her with his projects, which bored her to distraction.

He took a drag of his cigarette and exhaled as he asked, 'Do you have something to show *me*?'

'I don't know what you mean,' she replied, turning away. She was quite put off by his obvious leer since he was usually so submissive with her. Then she froze when she thought she felt his hand caress the cheeks of her bottom in her smooth cotton slacks.

'Don't you have *this* to show me?' he whispered in her ear.

She spun around to face him again. 'How dare you? I have never...! If I say one word of this to...'

'Sidney?' Albert kept his hand resting almost possessively on her bottom.

She slapped it away.

'I can also talk to Sidney, Mandy, my darling,' he threatened quietly, and now his hand rose to her lightly powdered cheek.

She wanted to bite him as his hand dropped to her neck, and kept moving slowly downwards. 'I don't know what you're talking about, Albert,' she said innocently, 'and I don't understand what's gotten into you.' She moved hastily away from him towards the desk.

'I'll be happy to show you.' He strolled lazily after her.

Amanda desperately scanned the surface of the desk for something to restore order, such as a photograph of her and Sidney together. What she found instead was a scattering of colourful and extremely graphic eight-by-tens. The photographs had captured particularly hot moments in an encounter between a high-school friend of hers, and a woman clearly identifiable as Amanda Vanforth, in all her naked glory. Her pale cheeks turned crimson as she saw several close-ups of her face, and her expression in the pictures made it clear she was in the throes of an orgasm. The man responsible for her pleasure was clearly not her husband. The man in the obscene images with her was Paul, and his hands were just where Albert's hand was now. Her brother-in-law was touching her bottom again, this time patting it in a gentle imitation of what Paul had been doing to her. The photographs showed her high school friend spanking her. She suffered a flush of feeling remembering the hard and passionate way Paul had fucked her that night, but then her mind returned to the present as Albert patted her right cheek, and then her left cheek, slowly, with no sense of urgency.

'Do you still want to talk to Sidney, Mandy?' he asked quietly.

'Don't call me that,' she snapped, but she didn't move away from his hand. 'How did you...?'

'Your friend is quite a professional,' he remarked, and pressed his hand against the cloth between her cheeks. She gasped as he fingered the deep valley dividing her buttocks through the tightly stretched cotton, feeling for her anus. She shifted her weight, trying to escape his intrusive caress, yet she didn't actually move away from him. She was too scared. 'He... did this?'

'Did this? Mandy, I tracked him down for this. Of all the guys in your high school yearbook, he was the only one who had a heart drawn around his face.'

'You stole my yearbook?' she exclaimed, turning to face him again. It surprised her how close he was, so close she could feel his heat. He was wearing a white shirt and tie, and the growing bulge in his black trousers gave her the panicky feeling that he wasn't wearing any underwear.

'I had to get a hold of this, Mandy.' He smiled again, and slid his hand up from her bottom to cup her left breast. She didn't move as he fondled her bosom, but she shuddered inside. In all the years she had known him, he had never before smiled at her like that. It was an ugly smile, the smile of a man who believes he owns something, and who is not necessarily gentle with his possessions.

'What do you want?' she asked, even though she knew.

'Well, Mandy,' he took a final drag from his cigarette, and put it out in the glass ashtray on his desk, 'we can start with you slipping your slacks down.'

Mandy stood with her hands clutching her ankles, trying to keep her balance while Albert's hands wandered up from her bare calves to her trim thighs and from there up to her bottom, where one of them stroked gently between her cheeks. Then he reached down around her and cupped both her naked breasts. 'Mandy?'

'Mm?' By now she knew that if she did not reply when he called her this, he would slap her bottom.

'Would you like to see Paul again?' he asked softly. His hands returned to her hips, and moved down to her silky thighs.

'Would I!' She wanted to kill the bastard.

'Good,' Albert said. 'Come in, Paul.'

She immediately straightened up out of her humiliating position, just in time to see Paul, her long-lost crush, enter Albert's office. It seemed to her that he was wearing the same suit she had last seen him in. He had put it on after fucking her, for well over an hour, in a motel room, apparently with a camera hidden in the closet. It was humiliating in the extreme to have him see her like this now, as shamelessly naked as she was when he left her, years ago. She had loved Paul. She had worshipped Paul. She had drawn hearts around his name in her yearbook as she imagined being married to him and taking his cock anywhere he wanted to put it.

That was before she became more realistic and married for money. Now she covered her mound with one hand and tried to hide her breasts with the other, but they were much too big.

'Don't bother.' Albert slapped her bottom.

Paul looked amused.

She blushed even more deeply.

'Paul,' her husband's brother said, 'take off your trousers.'

'Paul, how could you?!' she cried, and then looked at her brother-in-law, realising what he'd just said. 'Take off his trousers?' She didn't understand; she could not let herself understand.

'I needed the money,' Paul replied, and began slipping off his suit. 'I'm sure you'd sell anyone you knew if you had to,' he added cynically, sliding his black trousers down and exposing strong, tanned legs that still made her go weak in the belly. She had spent hours watching those legs running across the football field in shorts, and in track-suit bottoms. She had fallen in love with those legs from afar.

'I don't understand,' she said, still trying desperately not to. She had believed she could love Paul. When he had fucked her, it felt like heaven.

20

'What's not to understand, my dear?' Albert said as Paul's beautiful cock sprang free of his shorts. 'Get on the floor and suck him.'

'No!' Amanda Vanforth refused vehemently. 'Absolutely not!'

'Do you want to go back to living like you did before you married Sidney?' Albert whispered in her ear. His hand was burrowing deep between her buttocks, and she could feel one of his fingers threatening to probe inside her little rear hole.

'No,' she moaned. She couldn't possibly go back. She couldn't. She stared at Paul's cock... he had finally called her the last week of school, and less than two hours after they met for lunch she was on her back and panting from the pleasure of feeling his hard-on inside her.

'Kiss it,' Albert demanded.

She saw Paul's erect dick, so long and so thick, and bent towards it; she couldn't help herself. She took it into her mouth with a choked cry as Albert spanked her, and then suddenly he was pulling open the cheeks of her bottom, and *his* cock, which she had never felt or tasted before, was pushing its way into her rectum. She groaned. She had not taken even Paul's cock this way, and she tried to look up into his eyes as Albert penetrated her, but his eyes were closed as he bucked back and forth in and out of her mouth. It wasn't long before his handsome features twisted in a frown, and she nearly gagged as a torrent of hot spunk flooded her mouth and poured down her throat, just as Albert yanked her hips back, pressing her buttocks tightly against his humid groin, and came deep in her bottom.

After the two men had come, Amanda was forced to kneel on all fours while Albert spanked her. He said he wanted to be just like Paul, who stood by watching as her brother-in-law methodically smacked one of her cheeks, and then the other. He spanked her slowly and rhythmically, and when her buttocks were hot as an oven, they both took her again just like before, only this time she sucked Albert's cock while Paul slid his huge dick between her flaming cheeks and fucked her bottom.

He leaned over her to massage her breasts and finger her clitoris, and she was horrified when she started coming even though he was pulling all the way out of her burning hole to ram himself cruelly through her ring every time. She moaned in the throes of an utterly humiliating orgasm as Albert, smiling triumphantly, shot almost contemptuous trickles of sperm into her gasping mouth.

Later that night Amanda was sitting in her bath again, this time soaking her aching bottom and thinking that at least she might be able to start seeing Paul again now. She caressed her vulva with a bar of soap trying to wash away the memory of Albert, but she kept seeing his smile as he came in her mouth, and despite the steaming hot bathwater, she shivered.

At Amanda's high school reunion later that year - which Albert insisted she attend even though Sidney, thank goodness, was not going - Amanda sat between Paul and her brother-in-law. Albert had not graduated the same year they had, yet he had insisted on coming and seemed delighted to be there.

He wore a sleek tuxedo, and Paul wore that same suit of his. She was dressed - again at Albert's insistence - entirely in white. Her breasts swelled half out of a white sweater's extremely low neckline, her white skirt reached only halfway down her slim thighs, and her beret was also as white as snow. They were attracting all sorts of stares where they sat together, mostly from men since, for some reason, very few women had shown up for the reunion.

Finally the lights went out and the slideshow began, the *Where are they now?* part of the evening.

Mandy's nerves started tingling when she heard the announcer's voice booming loudly through the microphone, 'Tonight, as a special treat for all of you invited to this special preview of the actual reunion taking place tomorrow, we have a video presentation of the life-and-times of our very own Prom Queen, the girl voted most likely to succeed. Yes, we have special footage of the girl who made it all the way to the top, our very own Mandy Van, now New York's infamous Amanda Vanforth!'

She felt her body go cold with shock as on the big screen she suddenly saw a huge, naked version of herself being happily fucked in the ass by Albert while she happily sucked Paul's huge cock. The camera had been focused on her face; there was no doubt about the fact that the girl in the picture was her.

The slides clicked on remorselessly, one after another, and each one was worse than the last. Especially humiliating was a close-up of Paul spurting cum over her closed eyes, immediately followed by one of Albert pressing her face against the floor and making her lick it clean of sperm.

The terrible distorted voice through the microphone spoke again, and suddenly she realised it was her husband, Sidney, who was addressing the mostly male gathering. 'Yes, friends, your dear Mandy has been committing adultery. I'm sure that won't stand her in good stead through her divorce proceedings. And then, of course, there's the little matter of embezzling company funds for that little stock portfolio of hers she has put away for a rainy day. But let me tell you, folks, her husband knows about Amanda's little ways. Or should I say, Mandy's? Her husband has that portfolio well in hand, unlike Mandy. She really shouldn't have tried to cheat her husband. And that's why we're here now, ladies and gentlemen. You all have your lottery tickets? Well then, come on up, because one of you lucky ticket holders, as you all know from your invitations, gets to fuck Mandy Vanforth. One of you gets to fuck her any way you like, and another lucky winner gets to have her suck his cock. Come up, come up, one and all, and bring your tickets! Mandy?'

In a dream, Mandy found herself rising. 'Yes, Sidney?' she answered the god-like voice. She could not see beyond the lights of the slide machine that continued to project her giant face, and the circle of her rouged lips as she opened her mouth wide, straining to take Paul's cock deep inside.

'Why don't you show everyone just what they've won here today, Mandy? Take off your top.'

Still moving in a dream that was slowly and inevitably becoming the nightmarish realisation that she had lost everything, Mandy began pulling off her tight sweater. It got stuck around her forehead, and suddenly she found herself blind and helpless, her naked breasts exposed as she struggled to get it off over her head. Yet she could still hear that demonic voice through the sweater's soft folds.

'Isn't she lovely, folks? Aren't you glad you came to this pre-reunion? Hasn't the prize held its value over the years? Look at those breasts, still so firm. Isn't her husband a lucky man? Well, he wants to share his luck with all of you tonight.'

A hand grabbed her bottom suddenly, and then another one. She recognised Albert's pawing and Paul's more welcome grip, but then a strange hand grabbed one of her breasts and squeezed it. She jumped it was such a shock, but after that she went strangely still. She stopped struggling to get the top over her head as she felt another pair of unknown hands on her hips, and now someone else was lifting her skirt. A rough palm thrust itself between her thighs while gentler fingers pulled her panties down her legs. She just stood there while more and more hands felt her up, until she lost her balance, and then she sank to her knees.

Blindfolded by her top, Mandy got fucked in the ass again, this time with her breasts pressed against the cold floor as hands pulled her head up by the hair so another cock could slip into her mouth. She parted her lips for it, and when she felt sperm pouring down her throat, she swallowed that too. She shuddered as she felt one hard-on slip out of her bottom and another take its place, surging into her sperm-slicked back passage the second it became available. She thrust her buttocks up into the air, making it easy for rampant cocks to find their way between her cheeks and into her hot rectum. She shuddered, feeling yet more sperm spurting into her rear passage, but her cry was cut off as another penis slid into her gaping mouth.

She crouched on all fours and waited for the next erection, and the next, the cold tiles pressing against her breasts as the milk of countless men flooded her anus and her mouth, trickling out between her cheeks and down her chin. She didn't move, she just took what she had coming to her without trying to get away. She accepted this was how it had to be now as she lifted her hips to meet the new cock that drove into her so hard she felt as though it pierced her heart. She took the cock from behind and she took the cock in her face and nearly choked swallowing more mouthfuls of sperm, and when her mouth was emptied for an instant she cried, 'Come on, fuck me! I'm a slut! Fuck me!' She groaned as another pair of rampant dicks filled her up in breathtaking unison, and then she started laughing silently, her shoulders shaking in rhythm with the penises pulsing inside her, because she was Mandy Van again, just plain old Mandy Van getting fucked like a tart with nothing left to lose.

A Rope of Pearls

Mr McAllister bought his wife a string of pearls that she could only wear naked. If she wanted to wear them with clothes, or in front of people, there would be consequences. What these consequences would be, he did not say, but the way he smiled when he mentioned them gave Mrs Penny McAllister a tightening sensation in the pit of her stomach.

It all came to a head one Sunday when some friends of Penny came over for a visit. Amanda was there, and so were Caroline and the redheaded Susan. They were all attractive, single women in their thirties except for Penny, who had married a man a good deal older than her. She had met him on a course on computer administration. He had smiled at her, and offered to buy her coffee. She had accepted his invitation, and three months later they were married. That was when he gave her the pearls.

It was a long string of fresh-water pearls, white as shark's teeth and beautifully luminous. She wore the necklace, and nothing else, for him their first night together. She modelled it for him, slightly embarrassed by the fact that it hung down past her pussy. No matter how she wore the pearls, in one long loop, or wrapped several times around her neck so they fell over her pert and equally creamy breasts, she always felt more naked with them than without them. And at first, when he gave them to her at the restaurant, she had thought he was joking about the consequences of wearing them with clothes.

'What?' she had laughed at his warning. 'Oh, really? What would you do to me if I put them on right here?'

'There's only one way to find out, my dear,' he replied, smiling at her over his wine.

And so she did, she lifted the heavy necklace out of its box, in which it rested in luminous spirals against the crimson velvet lining, and slipped it on over her head. The pearls felt wonderfully cool against the bare skin of her neck and chest, and even then, dressed in an elegant black dress in a crowded restaurant, they made her feel so sensual she may as well have been naked.

Andrew's stare was penetratingly intense. 'Tonight, my dear,' he warned quietly, 'you'll find out.'

Meeting his eyes, she felt a tremor of fear in her belly mingled with excitement. Sex with Andrew McAllister had always been functional, competent; he got her off, but there was no... well, there was no danger involved. She never felt like she might lose control of herself when he touched her. But in the restaurant that night, a long string of pearls around her throat and his hand caressing her arm, and then her thigh beneath the table, she suddenly suffered the feeling of being owned, and she liked it.

When they got home later, the second she crossed the threshold of their large, five-bedroom house, she heard his voice just behind her say, 'Take everything off, my dear.'

She glanced back at him. 'I'm sorry?'

'Strip.'

The front door was open and a cold breeze was blowing into the house. 'Let's get to the bedroom first,' she said.

'I said, strip.'

'But Andrew...'

'You accepted the terms when you accepted my gift. If you do not wish to honour our agreement, I will be perfectly happy to dissolve our union.'

'Andrew...' She told herself he was joking even though part of her knew he wasn't.

'Do you keep your word?' he asked coldly.

'Andrew, I'm sorry, but...'

'Are you a woman of your word?'

She felt the beginnings of a sweet submissiveness that made her knees feel strangely weak; she had never experienced anything like this before.

'Do you want to live in this house, Penelope?'

'Yes,' she answered quietly.

'Then strip right here in the doorway.'

As he stood there in his black coat, hopefully blocking the view for anyone who happened to pass by on the pavement, she pulled her little black dress up over her head.

'Everything,' he insisted quietly.

She reached behind her, and unhooked her bra. She hesitated then, but his expression gave her the impetus she needed to slip it off, leaving her only in her pink cotton panties and her black garter belt and stockings.

'The rest,' he said relentlessly.

She could sense there was no arguing with him as the pink buds of her nipples stiffened in the cold, and yet she still hesitated.

'Your arse, Penny.'

She blushed; she hated to hear him use such language. Nevertheless, she pushed her panties down her thighs, and the pearls hung heavily from her neck as she bent over to step out of them. Then she was standing in the doorway wearing just her garter belt and stockings, facing the street where the late evening traffic was only just beginning to die down. Her blonde bush was visible to the world, and her breasts thrust perkily out into the night for all to see. The pearls felt cool against her flesh and teased her clitoris as the heavy strand rose and fell slightly with her quickening breaths. And she realised then that her pussy was getting wet, seriously wet, obeying her new husband like this against her own modest instincts.

'Now,' Andrew said, abruptly turning her around so she was facing the inside of the house and her naked bottom was exposed to the street, 'exercise for me.'

'Excuse me?' Penny was sure she must be dreaming, but unfortunately she was not. Burning with shame, she not only had to stand in the open doorway wearing only stockings and pearls, she had to bend over and touch her ankles. She was forced to spread her legs a little to do so, which pushed her naked bottom out towards the night and anyone who happened to be passing by.

She felt the frigid air invade her private parts, and the cold, hard pearls kiss her nipples as she stretched. Then Andrew turned her around so she was facing the street again, and when she bent over again, he thrust his erection inside her and fucked her swiftly and remorselessly from behind.

Yet he pulled out without coming, and she moaned as he replaced his delicious penis with one of his fingers. Her breath caught when she felt him transfer some of her hot juices from her pussy to the little puckered hole leading into her anus, and she closed her eyes in horror when he pulled her cheeks apart. He fucked her bottom with almost brutal energy, shoving his helmet through her ring and filling her with him as her cries of mingled pain and pleasure were drowned out by the sound of traffic rushing by in the street.

When he was finished with her - after he came with a great yell, yanking her buttocks up hard against him to ram his pulsing, spurting cock deep into her - she whimpered as he pulled out slowly. Then he helped her stand up straight, closed the door behind them, and crooked a finger under her chin so she was forced to look up into his eyes.

'There,' he said, 'this good girl deserves her hot bath now. And remember,' he added as she started eagerly up the stairs of her new home, surreptitiously wiping away her tears, 'anytime you want to wear those pearls again in front of anyone, you just let me know.' And he smiled.

That fateful night when her girlfriends came to visit, they were all rather tipsy from indulging in one drink too many. Amanda was getting married, and they were having a final girls' night out for her. They wound up at Penny's and Andrew's place after the club because it was a nice big comfortable house, not a small cramped apartment like the one's her single friends lived in. At two o'clock in the morning they were still chatting happily in the living room when Andrew came downstairs in one of his elegant robes. 'What's all this?' he asked.

The three friends, in various states of disrepair, were sprawled across the sofa, and in one of the big comfortable armchairs. Penny leapt to her feet the second Andrew entered the room, but her friends didn't bother to get up.

'Penny's been giving me a send-off to wedded bliss,' Amanda declared in a slurred voice. Being the party girl, she was the most sloshed.

'Yeah,' Caroline chimed in, 'tomorrow she's swearing to love, honour and obey. Fat chance!' If she hadn't laughed after she said that, maybe everything would have turned out differently. But she did laugh, and suddenly Penny knew the night was about to turn sour on her. She was trying to give Caroline a warning look when she heard Andrew's chillingly reasonable tone.

'Funny you should say that, Caroline, as Penny took the same oath. Didn't you, my pet?'

His tone alarmed her as much as it had the night she remembered all too well when he took her in the doorway both ways. 'Mm,' she murmured noncommittally, not liking the drift of this at all.

'Have any of you ever seen a demonstration of what that oath involves?' Andrew inquired pleasantly.

'I say, do you have a kinky streak, Pen?' Amanda giggled. 'You dirty thing, you!'

'Amanda, you will find that Penelope is not *into* anything,' Andrew said quietly. 'But she does have her perks, don't you, my dear? Have you shown them your pearls? Have you shown them the lovely gifts I give you?'

At the mention of the pearls, a crimson flush spread over Penny's face and her whole body seemed to get hot.

'Look at her!' Caroline exclaimed. 'Oh, this must be dirty!'

'Not at all,' Andrew assured her, 'it is merely a jewel, Penelope's private jewel. Isn't that so, my love?'

Penny felt her stomach turning. Since that night in the doorway she had stepped softly around Andrew and kept those pearls hidden safely away in a drawer. She only pulled them out when he asked her to wear them in bed for him. And then he caressed her bottom very gently before fucking her in the pussy as courteously as he usually did. Now, however, she felt her bowels stirring anxiously. 'It's a very *private* jewel,' she said finally.

'Why don't you fetch it, my pet?' Andrew suggested. 'Let's give the girls a full, live demonstration of what it means to love, honour and obey your husband.'

Flushed from head to toe, Penny fled the room, but it was upstairs she ran, to fetch her pearls. She knew she did not have a choice even as she reassured herself that he couldn't possibly mean to do anything to her in front of her friends. Yet the sound of laughter downstairs told her this was not a dream; this was happening. She lifted out the box she had hidden beneath her undergarments in the bottom drawer of her cabinet. Inside it, lying against the plush red lining, was the cool white string of pearls.

With an anxious tightness in her bottom, she walked slowly as a schoolgirl bound for punishment, back down the carpeted stairs.

Caroline was smoking when she came in and laughing at something Andrew had said. Susan was lying sprawled on her side on the other end of the sofa, asleep. Her husband was sitting between them.

'Bring it in Penny,' he said, 'and stand right here in front of us where we can see you.'

'Oh,' Caroline smiled at her, 'you aren't half kinky on the sly, are you, Pen? I didn't know you were like this.'

'You've not seen much of Penny's dark side, have you?' He smiled at her.

'Not for lack of trying,' Caroline replied, and returned his smile.

'You don't surprise me.' He looked back at his wife, who was standing a little unsteadily before him, holding the box clasped over her chest as if it might keep him and his intentions at bay.

'Show them what's in the box, Penelope,' he instructed firmly.

'Do I have to?' she asked, even though she knew what he would say.

'Do you remember what I offered you the last time we discussed the issue of whether or not you were a woman of your word, Penelope?'

'But I haven't *worn* them,' she protested.

'Oh,' Caroline looked delighted, 'this is good!'

'Would you like to see Penny's best jewel?' Andrew asked her.

'Would I!'

'There you have it, my dear. I think you should show your friends what domesticity means. I think it is your duty, as the only married woman in this room, to show them just what it means to love, honour and obey a man.'

'But I don't *want* to wear the pearls,' Penny insisted in a whining voice. She could feel matters slipping irrevocably out of her control.

'Open the box,' Andrew commanded.

She obeyed him, of course. The white pearls glowed against the deep red velvet, and at sight of them, a hush fell over the room.

'So?' Caroline finally asked.

'You know what to do now, Penelope,' her husband said.

Penny stood rooted to the spot as she felt all the air being sucked out of her lungs. There was a long pause, during which even Caroline held her tongue, and then with a resigned sigh, Penny felt the last of her resistance drain out of her. She set the box down on the coffee table, and without further ado, pulled her blouse up over her head. She was not wearing a bra, so her breasts sprang free.

Caroline's eyes latched hungrily onto her friend's lovely, perky bosom. Fortunately, Susan was half asleep and didn't see anything.

'Go on,' Andrew said softly.

She slowly raised her skirt. Her thighs were veiled in white stockings held up by a matching garter belt.

'Can I help her?' Caroline asked abruptly.

Not surprisingly, Andrew responded, 'I don't see why not.'

She rose from the couch and sank to her knees in front of Penny, who blushed even more deeply. Caroline's hands were soft and skilful; they quickly flicked up the clasps on her garter belt and pulled her stockings down with a swift, caressing gesture. 'And the rest?' She glanced back at Andrew for permission. It was as though she realised her friend, whom she had lusted after for so long in secret, had no will of her own now and was hers for the asking if she was simply polite to this man.

'If you like,' Andrew said magnanimously. 'It's called obedience.'

'Oh, I see that.' Caroline smiled and turned back to Penny, who could not bring herself to meet her eyes as her friend's light fingers quickly slipped into the sides of her white panties, and tugged them down to expose her soft blonde bush. At sight of it, Caroline seemed to grow impatient, because Penny nearly lost her balance as she tugged her panties down her legs, forcing her to step out of them quickly to keep her footing. Now she was completely exposed.

'Very nice,' Caroline said as she stood up, and apparently accidentally placed a hand on one of her friend's bare shoulders to steady herself.

Penny shivered as she felt something like an electric current tingle through her naked body at the other woman's touch.

'Is there more?' Caroline asked, gazing at Penny's down-turned gaze even as she addressed Andrew.

'Is there more, Penny?' he asked her in turn. 'Why don't you show them what more you do for me?'

'What would you like?' his wife asked submissively. She barely recognised her own voice it sounded so faint and dreamy. Part of her felt as if she was watching a snowy evening through a thick-paned window, so that she only saw how mysteriously beautiful it was without feeling the dangerous cold.

'Come and kneel before me,' her husband commanded gently.

She looked at him. He couldn't mean...

'Kneel right here.' He pointed at the floor between his knees.

He did mean it.

Caroline was still standing beside her, facing away from Andrew and smiling knowingly at her. It was an evil grin, one she usually showed only when talking about men. 'You *are* a good girl, Pen,' she said softly.

'I don't...' Penny protested weakly.

'You will kneel,' her husband said. 'She's seen it all before.'

'Not her, I haven't,' Caroline pointed out. 'She's my special friend.'

'I can't, not in front of...' Penny felt light-headed. She was still blushing from the memory of Caroline's hands lingering on her legs, which had made her feel so strange...

'Would you rather I had you kneel before Caroline? She's the one you wanted to demonstrate obedience to. Or perhaps we should wake Susan and teach *her* a lesson.'

'I'm fine...' Susan mumbled, without opening her eyes.

Penny walked past the smiling Caroline, and nearly felt her legs give way in front of Andrew; she had to put her hands on his knees to steady herself.

'You know what to do,' he said.

She glanced down at the bulge clearly visible beneath his robe that told her his cock was already almost fully erect.

Caroline sat down beside Andrew again and leaned against his shoulder, bringing her face down close to the knot in his belt. 'Show me what you can do, Penny,' she said, and leered at her as she licked her lips in anticipation.

Penny swallowed hard thinking of her suitcase upstairs and of her life in this house. Then she slipped her hands into her husband's dressing gown, found his hard-on, pulled it out gently, and put her lips to it as her friend giggled and reached out to stroke her hair.

Andrew looked on patiently, his hand coming to rest on Caroline's thigh as he said, 'Good girl... good girl...' while Penny worked her mouth up and down on his tool, her head bobbing in his lap. Then she gave a small, choked cry when he suddenly gripped the back of her head with one hand and pushed her face down hard over him as he came, pumping his white-hot cum down her throat and making her swallow every last drop. Finally he let her go, but only to punish her for taking so long to get the pearls.

Bent naked over a chair, Penny bit her lip as Andrew dangled the string of pearls from one hand while gripping the back of her neck with the other to hold her down. Then he brought the rope of pearls up in a slow arc, and each one stung painfully into her buttocks as he lashed her with it. She was stunned to discover how like a whip a string of pearls could feel, how like a long and cruelly knobbed whip raising a string of red welts across her exposed bottom and making her squeal.

'If you don't take your strokes like a good girl,' he warned, 'we'll have to start all over again, only this time we'll do it outside on the pavement. Or you could, of course, leave with Caroline and never return to this house again.'

Penny closed her eyes and stifled a moan as she waited for the rope of pearls to bite her bare cheeks again.

After he had finished punishing her with the pearls, her husband made her crouch down on the floor, the infamous necklace around her neck, her cheek pressed against the carpet and her elbows chaffing against it as her bottom was pummelled, regularly and repeatedly, by a ten-inch dildo wielded with great enthusiasm by her friend, Caroline, who was naked now except for the strap-on she always carried around in her purse, just in case she got lucky. Caroline thought this was a great way to express friendship as well as obedience. Andrew stood by watching, and Susan was no longer asleep.

She was sitting up straight, her dress bunched around her waist while she eagerly stroked her clitoris and slipped two fingers up into her pussy, which was getting unbelievably hot watching her friend being banged from behind by her other friend. She was looking forward to her wedding tomorrow even more now, and the oath she would take to love, honour and obey her husband, no matter what.

The Presenter Presented

Erica Johnson was a large-breasted blonde with a contrastingly thin waste and a mane of long golden curls she tossed to great effect in the presence of men, and since she worked in television, it could be said she was always in the presence of men and performing for them.

At the moment she was fiddling with one of the buttons of her blouse, which showed off the beautiful breasts she seldom imprisoned in a bra. She was riding in the glass elevator all the way to the top of the Television Tower building, and she was nervous because the boss had asked to see her. This was not in itself an unusual occurrence; he had asked to see her before. She had been to see Chairman Mathews dozens of times with at least two buttons undone on her blouse, a ploy that always worked when she had to deal with difficult men. But this time was different.

Erica had a reputation for trouble. When you had breasts the size of hers and a pretty smile and gorgeous hair and you liked to laugh, well, people just looked at you. She had found the perfect job for herself as a sports broadcaster and a sports show hostess. The trouble was that Erica enjoyed being looked at off camera as well. She liked it so much that she often wound up in the newspapers, for one reason or other. And she had the unfortunate habit of getting involved with men who liked to tell afterwards, or who were not very discreet. One of these men had taken her to a topless beach, where a photographer had secretly snapped their picture, and the following morning her naked breasts graced the front page of several tabloids in all their glory. Millions of people had gazed at them over milk and cornflakes and jammy toast. Which was why she was a little nervous this time about going to see Chairman Mathews. She was just a bit concerned that, this time, she had gone too far. Not that it was her fault, she told herself as she flicked open one more button on her white blouse, but people never understood that. Naturally, he could not fire her, but she freed one more button just in case. It was the last button she could undo and still sport a professional aura rather than look like a total slut.

She was very popular, she reminded herself in the mirror just outside the chairman's door. Men liked her, women envied her, and all that had to be worth something. She wiped a stray blonde curl out of her eye with a manicured finger, and knocked quietly on the double mahogany doors.

There was no answer.

She knocked again, and almost immediately one of the doors swung in on silent hinges. No one seemed to be in the suite, with its stunning view of the city below. No one was at the secretary's desk just outside the chairman's office. No one was here at the nerve centre of commercial television where the most important phone, the phone that warned of any technical emergencies or news breaking stories, was hung.

Erica walked up to the desk feeling a little panicked. She had expected to plead for her job, not to be so unimportant as to be stood up.

'Ah, Erica,' a voice said from somewhere behind her, and she recognised it as Chairman Mathews's. Apparently, it had come from a bathroom tucked discretely away between the oak panelling and bookshelves lining the suite's chestnut walls. As she turned, a section of mock bookcase swung open and revealed her boss with his bald head and his slight paunch contained in a blue shirt that matched his striking eyes. And Erica could not believe her own eyes, because the chairman was on the toilet. But then, as she stared at him in horror, she realised that he was not actually on the toilet, meaning he was not using it for its intended purpose. His shining black trousers were crumpled round his ankles and he was sitting on the lid of the toilet while his secretary, an older woman with her hair gathered up in a bun at the nape of her neck, knelt on the floor before him with his penis buried in her mouth.

The chairman was being sucked off!

'Won't be a minute, Erica,' he said. 'Come over here, I'd like you to see something.'

In a daze, Erica approached the doorway of the tiny bathroom. Her heavy breasts swayed back and forth inside her blouse as she walked, but she was scarcely aware of them any more. She paused just outside the doorway as the chairman grabbed hold of his secretary's head, and guided it into moving more swiftly up and down his erection. 'You see, Erica... look at me while I'm speaking to you,' he demanded.

31

She looked at him. Now he was caressing his secretary's tightly contained hair. The woman didn't look up, she was much too busy, and Erica couldn't tell if she minded being seen like this. She certainly didn't seem to mind what she was doing.

'Look at me,' the chairman repeated.

Erica forced herself to meet his eyes. They were a chilling blue that made her shiver somewhere deep in her belly, and she realised that was why she didn't like looking at him. The way he made her feel wouldn't help her get her way during negotiations.

'You see, Erica, this is private business. What Miss Brown is doing to me - suck Miss Brown, suck, that's good - is private. We all do this sort of thing behind closed doors... I said, look at me, Erica.'

Her eyes had wandered again; she found it intensely humiliating having to look at his cock disappearing in and out of the kneeling woman's mouth. She wondered why that was, why she minded what the other woman was doing. But he was talking again, and it was important she listen to what he was saying, that she not let the sight of his rigid, gleaming shaft distract her...

'We do it in private, Erica, whereas you do it in print.' Suddenly, he reached up and grabbed one side of her half open blouse.

Automatically Erica moved forward to prevent him for tearing the fine material and fully exposing her breasts, and before she knew it, she found herself bending over his face, between him and his secretary's bobbing head.

'Do you like doing things in public, Erica?' he asked sternly.

'No Mr... I mean, Chairman Mathews, no...' she stammered, surreptitiously trying to get his grip off her blouse while politely trying to look back into his hypnotic eyes. Her hand brushed ineffectually at his sleeve.

'Do not touch me, Erica, not unless you want to touch me where *she's* touching me. Would you like to help out?'

'No!' Erica quickly dropped her hand as embarrassment added an attractive colour to her cheeks no make-up artist could ever emulate. Bent over him like this, her breasts were practically hanging out of her blouse in plain view of his face as she looked away from his penetrating stare again.

'Look at me, Erica,' he commanded.

She looked at him.

His other hand got a firmer grip on the back of his secretary's head, and he literally shoved her face down into his lap. The woman gave a muffled cry as he pulled her head back up by her tight bun, and then pushed it deep into his crotch again. His expression grew oddly stiff as he looked into Erica's wide eyes, but he made no sound as he came, there was only the muffled gulping of Miss Brown's frantic swallowing as Chairman Mathews pumped his cum into her demure little mouth and down her obedient throat. Meanwhile, Erica swallowed dryly as she watched, but her pussy was getting wetter by the second.

Then Chairman Mathews lifted Miss Brown's head off his still partially erect penis, and let her collapse back onto her efficient tweed skirt as he stood up. 'You like things public, don't you, Erica?'

'No,' she said quickly. More than ever, she had no idea where to look. His still hard prick bobbed up and down before him when he moved, a drop of sperm quivering on its cleft head, and she suffered the terrifying impression that he wanted *her* to lick it off. She felt dizzy suppressing the urge to sink willingly to her knees before it as she tried to keep a firm grip on the conversation.

'On your knees, Erica.'

'Sir,' she said weakly, 'I can explain about the photographs...'

'Do you want to keep working here, Erica?'

'Yes, sir,' she answered miserably.

'Then on your knees.'

'I have a contract...' she began, but she knew perfectly well that he could break any contract she had signed. Feeling two inches tall, she sank to her knees before him so his cock hung in the air directly in front of her face. The secretary did not look at her, and she too kept her eyes away from the other woman.

'Erica, pull my trousers up for me, please,' said the chairman.

Trying not to look at his prick as she did so, Erica pulled his sleek black trousers up for him, and then looked up as he zipped them closed just over her head.

'Erica, you don't understand boundaries. You don't understand boundaries because you have no experience of them. I will have to teach you what boundaries mean.'

Chairman Mathews was still talking, and Erica was still listening, only now she was naked. He had asked her to take her blouse off. Then he had asked her to take her skirt off as well. She had protested, despite a certain thrill at the thought of being seen by him, the same thrill that always, somehow, put her in the position to be caught by photographers doing something most people didn't get caught doing. This thrill was going to be the death of her...

'Do you want me to see only as much of you as the rest of the world has seen on the front page of the newspaper?' Chairman Mathews enquired acidly. 'If I didn't think you felt closer to me than you do to these anonymous readers, Erica, I would have to fire you, as it would be a pointed insult. However, if I felt there was some bond between us, a special intimacy that made you want to share something with me you haven't shown the whole world,' he sighed meaningfully, 'well, then, I might have an interest in keeping you around.'

She took a deep breath, and pushed her skirt down, letting it fall around her ankles so she could step out of it.

'And the rest,' he said. 'You show more than that on a tanning salon bench, Erica. Get on with it.'

She bit her lower lip, slipped her fingers into the sides of her bikini bottoms, and lifted them down off her blonde bush. She was still wearing the bikini bottoms from her midnight swim, the ones the photographer had caught her in, the bikini bottoms resting on breakfast tables everywhere this morning all across the country.

The chairman looked intently down at her mound, protected by lovely, curling blonde hair, and she knew better than to use her hands to try and cover herself.

And she *liked* him looking, that was the vexing thing. She had to suppress a wanton urge to grind her hips and sway towards him. But she did sway a little she felt so light-headed, and shifted her weight from one high-heel to another feeling like a little girl standing in front of a stern headmaster. She would be bumping and grinding in his face soon if she let herself go...

'At least now I know you're a natural blonde,' he remarked.

She tried to smile, but couldn't quite manage it.

'Sit in that armchair and keep your legs open,' he instructed.

She sat down demurely, and her blush deepened as she made herself obey his command to keep her legs spread. Then he told her to lift her thighs over the arms of the chair, and totally unsettled her. But she obeyed him, and wriggled her bottom against the firm cushion as he studied her most private parts. She had to struggle not to let her excitement get out of hand as she concentrated on what he was saying.

He was summing up her job. She was the lead presenter on a sports quiz show. Sports personalities were invited to appear, and were asked questions. It was her job to tell them if they had the right answer or if they had gotten it wrong. She had met quite a few men during the filming of the show that had gotten her into trouble later. 'I think that's what the problem is, Erica,' chairman Mathews concluded as he walked slowly back and forth in front of the chair on which she sat spread-eagled, keeping her gaping pussy in full view as he spoke. He never walked so far to one side that he could not keep looking straight at the exposed core of her feminine flesh, and she writhed beneath his assessing stare, unconsciously thrusting her vulva up towards his eyes. 'Your trouble is that you can't keep your hands off these men. You can't keep your hands off the players, my girl. But that's all right, it doesn't have to be a problem. You're just going to have to learn to go all the way, that's all.'

The secretary, thank God, had been sent out of the suite before he told her to strip, but now Erica began wondering if that was such a good thing after all. She could sense where this was going, and she wasn't sure she should do what her throbbing, begging pussy wanted. Her mind told her to put her legs together like a good girl and talk business. Her cunt wanted her to slide forward in the chair, raise her legs and shove her feet behind her head so he could *really* look.

Chairman Mathews was walking back and forth in front of her, staring at her, and she could see the sight was affecting him. In his trousers - the sleek black trousers she had watched him zip up only minutes ago - a new bulge was becoming visible. The prick she had helped him put away was getting stiff again as his eyes lingered on her spread cleft and her soft blonde pubic hair.

'What we'll do, Erica...' he paused, and abruptly stopped pacing to lean over her.

She shivered at how close he was, finally. Those bloody eyes! Why couldn't they be bloodshot and baggy? Your boss shouldn't have eyes like sapphires. It should be against the law!

'What we'll do,' he went on quietly, 'is let you have your fun, only we'll do it under the bright lights for all our viewers to enjoy.'

She looked breathlessly up into his gemstone-hard eyes. Was he going to touch her? Her mind was afraid of that new bulge in his trousers, but her body was thrilled by it. Her pussy was urging her to reach out and touch it to determine just how hard he was for her. He was looking deep into her eyes again. He hadn't done that since he came in his secretary's mouth. 'What do you mean... for the viewers?' she asked, even though she really couldn't think straight. She was too busy concentrating on not letting herself reach out for him. She could not let herself, that much she knew for certain, or she would lose any negotiating power she had left. If she kept wanting to touch him so much, she was going to end up doing whatever he told her to...

'You'll do it for your viewers,' he said. 'You like to be seen, don't you?'

'Do what, sir?'

'What you're doing for me.'

Her eyes widened in disbelief. 'What?'

'When they answer the questions correctly,' he elaborated, 'this is what they win.'

Erica looked up at him, not letting herself understand. The bulge in his trousers shifted slightly to the left. She could just put one hand out and trace its shape through the soft material...

'We'll air the show later at night, post watershed,' he informed her, and smiled down into her uncomprehending eyes. 'We'll get you a costume, some lovely lacy number that comes apart in bits.'

'I don't understand,' she said, even as the thought of wearing a stripper's outfit that came off easily, one seductive piece at a time, made her push her hips up off the chair.

'To make the show last, my pretty, the winners can be rewarded little by little for each question they answer correctly. First, they get to see this...' he grabbed her right breast, and squeezed it.

She gasped, and jumped in the chair from the totally unexpected pleasure of his sudden, possessive grip, and now all she wanted was for him to squeeze her other breast as well. 'And... and if they answer all the questions correctly?' she asked in a husky voice, concentrating hard on not returning his touch.

'That's just the start, my dear. When they've answered the first round, and your kit is all off, then they compete for positions.'

Erica struggled to stay seated upright in the chair. His face was looming directly over her face now, his breath mingling with hers, and she wanted his zipper down more than anything. 'Chairman Mathews, I'm sorry, I...'

'If you want to work in television ever again, Erica, you won't break our contract. You have to work for me no matter what I do to the format of the show, and I've decided on an adult format for our after-hours viewing audience. That's why I tested the public's reaction.'

'The public's reaction?' she asked, and gasped again as his hand moved down to her belly and lightly stroked her bush. His fingers lingered over it, tormenting her. If only he would only put them where they belonged, inside her!

'You see, Erica, all the pictures in the newspapers were *my* idea.' He smiled down at her again. 'I hired photographers to follow you.'

'It was *you*?' This admission of profiteering lust from him stripped the last vestige of professionalism from the interview, and suddenly she realised how utterly naked and helpless she was in every sense. Her whole being was as exposed and eager and greedy as the aching clit she longed to shove up into his mouth.

'It was me.' His smile deepened as his fingertips gently parted the lips of her pussy and slipped up her slick labia to her throbbing button. 'I know the public want to see more of you, so the sports stars get to fuck you live on television twice a week, the ones that win, that is. Only the ones that win are worth letting in, don't you agree?' And his hand started working on her.

'Oh, God, I can't... I mustn't...'

'You can, Erica, you're a natural. And speaking of winners,' he added, 'let's let the first one in right now. On the floor, my dear, on your front. I want to show you your new position here at the station. This is the position you'll assume when the champions screw you. You'll be a very flexible prize.'

'But...'

'Face down on the floor, Erica. I'm sure you've been taken that way before.'

'Not professionally...' she slipped out of the chair onto her knees.

'These young athletes know how to get it into the net,' the Chairman said, 'but it takes an older man to know what to do with it once it's been bagged.' He slipped off his black silk tie.

'What are you doing?' she asked in a trembling voice, she was so eager for him to do it, to feel him inside her.

'Put your hands behind your back,' he said.

'Is this in the contract?' she asked faintly.

'I'll have you spanked at the beginning of every show if you're not careful, Erica.'

Crouching forward, she put her hands behind her and felt him wrap the cool silk around her wrists twice before he tied a firm knot. She could scarcely believe she was kneeling at the foot of Chairman Mathews's chair with her bare bottom thrust up into the air. And suddenly, he hit her hard with the flat of his palm. The smacking sound of his hand coming down on her cheeks sounded incredibly loud in the wood-panelled room. 'Ouch!' she cried, because this was something new to her. None of the men she had been with had ever raised a hand to her like this. The smooth flesh of her bottom stung terribly, and a tremor of mingled fear and desire forked through her belly and welled up into her throat in the form of a long, passionate moan. She ground her hips up and back, desperate to feel his cock inside her.

'Would you like me to put that in your contract, Erica?' Chairman Mathews's eyes shone as he unzipped his trousers.

'I'll do whatever you say,' she replied huskily from deep in her throat, and closed her eyes as he raised his hand to spank her again, and again. Then her cries of pain tapered out into a low groan of longing when she finally felt his weight against her. Tears pricked the back of her eyes, tears of frustration that she had lost control of herself, but then she forgot everything except for the sensation of his hand stroking her pussy. His fingers were teasing her, and getting her even hotter and wetter than she already was, which hardly seemed possible. At the same time her tears dried up as she accepted the fact that she didn't have a problem with being the Chairman's slut, she didn't have a problem with it at all, in fact. She was a public girl and she liked to be noticed and she would be in the public eye a great deal from now on. She pressed her face against the expensive carpet as she thrust her buttocks up into the air for him, and stifled a moan of disappointment as he pulled her cheeks apart, and slowly pushed his erection into her bottom, bracing himself on her hips as he got what he wanted, and she got what she could never have asked for out loud. He banged her with a vengeance, his blue eyes blazing, and she came and came as she accepted her new position and began her new public career when Chairman Matthews came in her arse.

Her arse was such a lovely rose colour from the spanking that Chairman Mathews declared she would have to come visit him before every show, so her viewers would get to see the best her body had to offer in full glorious colour, and he would put this clause in her new contract. He said he would make sure she gave herself fully to her public as he squeezed her sore buttocks. She moaned, her mind reeling as she felt him step in front of her. Her lifted her head up by the hair, and made her lick his erection. And she did it, she willingly licked the cock that had just come out of her bottom. He patted her blonde curls approvingly, and then untied her hands and told her to crawl over to the little bathroom, where he handed her a sponge and rubber gloves and ordered her to clean the floor.

'You told me you would do anything I said,' he reminded her, casually slipping his tie back on.

Utterly dazed, Erica slipped on the pink latex gloves, picked up the sponge, and knelt down on all fours on the hard tiles.

'Here.' Suds splashed out of the tin bucket he shoved towards her with his foot. 'Now put some foam on your nipples, Erica, and turn to me at smile.'

She looked up at him without thinking, and the flash from a camera blinded her for an instant. The instamatic whirred, and a moment later Chairman Mathews was waving a drying print over her face. She saw a naked girl on her knees next to a bucket and a toilet, a sponge in her hand.

'Now be a good girl, Erica, or I'll have to put this picture in the papers and show the world what you really are, an obedient little scrubber, not the glamour queen everyone wants to fuck. Clean my toilet before you leave, please.'

And while Erica scrubbed, he took more pictures of her, focusing especially on the lovely round, glowing bottom that would soon be the star of the late show.

The Teacher Teased

Miss Smith was a schoolteacher in the last stretch of her first training year. She was blonde and pretty, her hair almost as short as a boy's, but her figure, more often than not exposed by tight T-shirts and jeans, made it abundantly clear she was a girl. Indeed, all the boys at her school, St Martin's on Tyne, never tired of looking at the shape of her lovely breasts nestling like perfect round apples beneath her blouse, with the stems of her nipples poking enticingly against the fine cotton. Nor did they tire of admiring her buttocks, tight as melons that made you want to squeeze them and dig your fingers into their soft warmth.

Miss Smith was on edge today, because although she was near the end of her teacher training year, this week was to be the crucial test of her pith, her stamina, and her authority over her charges. The week would begin when, alone with thirty boys and the headmaster, she would ride down to Readingly, another boys' school, for the annual Schools' Meet. The schools would compete against each other at cricket and all the other usual sports, which meant the boys would run about in the mud a lot. Normally more than one member of staff accompanied the headmaster to this event, but this time the school nurse had sprained a leg and begged off, saying the Readingly nurse would serve for both teams. And so the headmaster, a tall, greying and slightly forbidding man, smiled sweetly and told Miss Smith that it was just him and her. 'Just we two and the elements,' he said cheerfully.

'How lovely, headmaster.' She returned his smile even as her insides turned to jelly.

Everything went well until their first night away when the boys were sleeping in the Readingly dorm in the beds left vacant by other boys; the sports day was planned to coincide with other excursions, thus leaving the loud and rambunctious sixteen to eighteen-year-olds alone in the school. This meant there was an entire floor of approximately fifty beds occupied by sixteen to eighteen-year-old boys. The Readingly staff were reduced, since many of them had to go with the older boys on their own field trips.

On the night of Miss Smith's arrival with her loud and rambunctious charges, it was with some alarm that she realised her only professional companion, the headmaster himself, had been invited by the Readingly school's own headmaster to drink in the Readingly Library, with its fireplace and leather chairs and crystal decanted old port. The Readingly nurse went home to her cottage on the edge of the grounds, and the male staff were all away on field trips. This, with the two headmasters ensconced contentedly over drinks and a game of chess in the library, left Miss Smith in sole charge of fifty boys. The responsibility fell on *her* alone to somehow make sure they all stayed in their beds.

She didn't mind, really. Yes, there were the saucy comments from the older boys to deal with, after all, they *were* boys and randy as goats, but she didn't mind too much. She blushed a little as she felt their eyes devouring her breasts as she passed down the halls in school, but she wore tight T-shirts because she liked to be noticed. She enjoyed the power her curvaceous body gave her over the male breed. She even enjoyed catching their eyes on her bottom as she turned away from the blackboard during a lesson, or looked up from her marking at the desk to find some boy staring deep into the neckline of her blouse, and blushing red as beetroot when she met his eyes.

That was how she had first noticed Darren Coombes liked her. He was taller than most of the other boys, and more than most, he seemed a man at seventeen. She had seen him swimming once when she passed the school swimming hall, and as she paused to admire his well-muscled body, he had finished his lap and caught her staring at him. Then one day she had caught his gaze burning through her T-shirt during maths. She asked him if he could count beyond the number two, and he went the colour of ripe plums with embarrassment. Ever since then he had not looked her in the eye again, not until that first night at Readingly.

She had the advantage in the dorm, in that all the boys were sleeping in adjoining wings and the partitions had been pulled back between them to make patrolling and controlling the huge lot of young manhood more simple. She walked, holding a torch, down the corridor between the two long rows of beds, flashing the narrow beam of light here and there and occasionally catching a furtive face. The headmaster had made it clear he did not wish to be disturbed this evening, and he was not above dropping her final grade as a trainee teacher on the basis of something as stupid as being made to lose a game of chess against another headmaster. And then her wandering beam of torchlight hit upon a sheet that was clearly being agitated. The agitations took the form of an up and down motion which suggested a boy was doing something improper with himself. She flashed the light over the head of the bed, and was surprised to see Darren Coombes' face looking up at her with a leer, instead of with the mortified expression she had expected to see.

'Found something interesting, Darren?' she asked as insouciantly as she could. 'Still having trouble dealing with things that come in twos, I see.'

He didn't blush, and his stare did not waver from where it was fixed on her face.

'Put it away, Darren,' she said as firmly as she could without sounding too stern, 'or it'll fall off.'

'Why don't you put it away for me, miss?'

She was astonished. A bit of a fidget in the dark could be expected, but this insolence was inexcusable; she could not possibly let him get away with it. 'What did you say, Darren?' She was still whispering. She could not be sure how many boys within ear shot were still awake.

'Why don't you put my dick away for me, Miss Smith?'

'Keep your voice down!' she hissed. 'Are you aware of how much trouble you're in?' She made an effort to keep her own voice playful - he was, after all, only a horny boy, God bless him - but such presumption could not be tolerated.

'Are you aware,' Darren pulled himself up in the bed, his hand still pumping away beneath the sheet, 'of how much trouble *you* are in, Miss Smith, with a riot about to break out?'

She looked at him in consternation. He was almost a man, really, and with his hand still insolently going up and down under the sheet, the look in his eyes was worrisome. Yet what could he be talking about? Then a light hit her full in the face from across the room as someone else lit a torch. 'Who is that?' she demanded, but then another light hit her, and then another one. She was caught in a triangulated set of torch beams coming from three different sides of the dorm. And then a fourth torch came to life, and another one, and another one, until it seemed as if every boy had hidden a torch under his pillow. Miss Smith felt the blood rushing up into her face.

'Miss Smith,' Darren Coombes sighed.

'I demand to know what the meaning of this is!' she blurted. 'Darren, are you responsible for this... this...?'

'Rebellion?' He smiled up at her, and at least his hand stopped moving beneath the sheet. 'I wouldn't call it that, miss, not yet.'

'What are you talking about?' She told herself to remain calm. She had to remain calm. Too much was at stake here to panic.

'I'm talking about fifty boys wide-awake and in need of entertainment,' Darren explained. 'If you don't entertain us, we'll turn the place into a madhouse and disturb the headmasters.'

He would make a great negotiator one day, she thought wildly, suddenly disturbed instead of relieved by the fact that his hand was no longer pulling at his cock beneath the sheet. It made her wonder what he thought was going to touch his cock now instead of his hand. It made her mouth water against her will and her legs feel weak. 'What... what are you thinking of?' she muttered. The lights of a good forty to fifty torches were shining directly on her. She felt as though she was on stage beneath a hot spotlight trained directly on her. She could feel the subtle warmth of so many penetrating beams pricking the hairs on her bare arms, and almost caressing her breasts through her thin T-shirt like a very soft summer breeze.

'Strip,' Darren Coombes said.

Just one word and her whole universe was suddenly turned upside-down. She stood gaping at him in pure disbelief. Then all around her in the breathless silence, as she tried to absorb that one word, she heard fifty beds creak as fifty boys edged forward across the sheets. She could almost feel them all holding their breaths, waiting. 'You - you can't be serious,' she said.

No sooner had the words passed her lips than Miss Smith heard the first hand landing on the first bed frame with a clang of hollow steel tubing, followed by another clang as another hand fell to brace itself on another bed frame. Suddenly the dorm was becoming a dangerously loud percussion orchestra. And then the chant began, 'Strip! Strip! Strip! Strip! Strip! Strip!'

'Get your panties down for the lads.' Darren Coombes smiled up at her placidly over the growing noise. 'It's the least you can do, Miss Smith. After all, we've all behaved very well for you this year, haven't we, and fair's fair, isn't it? We scratch your back, you scratch ours.'

'Enough!' she cried.

The clanging continued as the chant 'Strip! Strip! Strip!' gradually became throatier, more of a threatening growl.

'You won't get us to be quiet any other way,' Darren warned her, somehow making his quietly firm voice audible to her over the commotion.

'No,' she gasped. 'I couldn't possibly!'

'Strip! Strip! Strip! Strip! Strip! Strip!'

'All right!' she screeched, suddenly prepared to do anything to stop all this dreadful noise. Any second now, she was sure, the headmaster would hear it and her career as a teacher would be over before it ever really began. She would cause him to lose his chess game and it would be proved that his staff could not control his pupils. She would be downgraded at the end of her year; she would not teach at St Martin's again. Perhaps she would never be able to teach *anywhere* again. She had to stop this terrible racket at once.

'All right,' she said again, more calmly.

Darren raised a hand, and a blessed silence fell over the dorm. Suddenly it was so quiet she could hear raindrops pattering softly against the windows. 'Your shoes first,' Darren said.

'What did you have in mind?' she asked, trying to sound casual and to buy herself some time to think about how she could get out of this very strange predicament she found herself in.

'Take your shoes off or we'll lose you your job.' Darren's tone was a slap in the face.

Blushing to the roots of her hair, she bent over to undo them, and her blush deepened as someone whistled at the sight of her bottom raised up into the air, now the avid target of the combined torchlight. She straightened up again quickly, and stepped out of her shoes. 'Is there anything else I can do for you?' She tried to smile, as if her heart wasn't racing and making it hard for her to think straight.

'Your shirt,' Darren said simply. 'Take it off.'

'What are you getting out of this, Darren?' She appealed to him directly. 'Don't you like me?'

'Oh, I like you all right, Miss Smith, I just want to see if I can like you even more. Don't you want to see how much better we can get along, Miss Smith?'

As she was trying to think of an answer, the laughter went out of his eyes.

'Your shirt,' he said again, flatly.

She reached to her belt, and tugged the bottom of her T-shirt out of her jeans. She heard the collective catching of over fifty breaths in anticipation as she reluctantly dragged the hem of her T-shirt up over her tummy, and then taking a deep breath herself, pulled it up to expose her bosom. She wasn't wearing a bra and she felt her breasts spring free, their soft nipples quickly stiffening a little in the cool air of the open dorm. 'There, is that all right?' Holding her shirt up, she squinted into the light blinding her as she showed off her stiffening breasts to over fifty pairs of avid eyes; to fifty boys who she knew would all love to fuck her; to fifty boys who wanted to screw her brains out one after the other... she new she was in trouble when she felt the unmistakable melting sensation in her pussy as it began to get dangerously wet.

'Take if off,' Darren insisted.

Without further protest, she pulled her shirt up over her face as she felt all their eyes, hungrily, ravenously devouring her naked torso. Then the shirt was off over her head and she had let it fall to the floor beside her.

'Now the jeans,' Darren said.

She looked at him again almost shyly, and started raising a protective hand towards her bare breasts.

'Drop it,' he said harshly.

She quickly lowered her hand, and trembling a little, she opened her jeans. She had to tug on the stiff metal zipper, and she cursed the tightness of the denim she had revelled in wearing to torment these boys, who now held her captive. It was that much harder to struggle out of, and she gave over fifty boys quite a show as she was obliged to bend over slightly, thereby sticking her bottom out again in order to push her jeans down her slender legs. There was a soft, collective sigh as the cheeks of her buttocks sprang free of the imprisoning denim.

Finally, she stepped out of her jeans and straightened up again. She was naked now except for a skimpy pair of white cotton panties that barely covered her ash-blonde bush, and she was blushing as deeply as Darren had that day in class when she humiliated him in front of his peers, perhaps even more deeply.

'Let's see you,' he said. He was speaking quite softly now as all the boys shone their torches right between her thighs. Fifty torch beams were aimed right at her pussy.

'Is there anything else...' she began without really knowing what she meant to say, 'I mean, do I really have to? It's so private. It's who I am...'

'This is who I am,' Darren said, and flung the sheet back to reveal a truly impressive hard-on that launched proudly up from his lap. Its thick length was a lovely pink with a warm purple tip, and it looked like it was positively aching to be taken in.

'What do you want me to... to do?' Miss Smith asked weakly.

'Do you want to show us what you are, and then show us what you do with what we are?' Darren asked quietly, almost respectfully, his eyes intensely earnest.

'What do you want?' she repeated desperately, helplessly, but she already knew, of course. She reached out her hand to him.

He grabbed her wrist and pulled her hand down, and over a hundred wide eyes watched as he forced her down onto her knees beside his bed. 'Show me,' he said, 'what you think of who I am.'

She looked at him, and he looked back at her where she cowered, nearly naked on the floor of a boys' dorm, and slowly lowered her face over the tumescent head of his beautiful cock. He groaned in anticipation, and fifty torches converged on her face as she parted her lightly painted lips and slipped his helmet between them. After that, there was no closing her mouth or turning back. She sucked Darren Coombes off in front of two sixth forms of teenage boys.

And that wasn't all she did. Although she sucked as gently as she possibly could, hoping to pull her mouth off in time, Darren gripped her neck firmly when his groin began pulsing, and to her horror, Miss Smith found herself swallowing mouthful after mouthful of her pupil's cum in front of all his peers. And then she fell flat on her bum next to his bed, her legs spread wide, when he pushed her away from him.

But she still had plenty more mortifications to endure. After Darren Coombes had come he made her take her panties off anyway, as she had known he would. Then he made her bend over the end of his bed as each individual boy stepped up to get a close look at her pussy. She held herself perfectly still while they each shone their torch right on her vulva, but didn't touch her. That was the deal, that there wouldn't be any touching. No one but Darren was allowed to touch her. The deal was that Miss Smith would bend over the bed while they all got a good long look at her quim, and then they would all get to watch while Darren fucked her, sitting on a chair, in the middle of the dorm.

First he took her from behind, still bent over the bed, then he sat down on the chair and she mounted him. After that she stood on a small table, also strategically placed in the middle of the dorm, as he fingered her pussy and subjected her to her first public orgasm.

Then Darren spanked her. 'Just to make it official who's teaching who, miss,' he said. She had no choice but to bend over the bed again and take ten of the best from Darren, administered one buttock at a time, with his slipper. The sound of the rubber sole smacking against her cheeks echoed through the dormitory as more than fifty boys counted the strokes out loud while she sobbed and bit the pillow to stifle her cries.

She was sure the headmaster would finally hear something as, after her punishment, Darren shoved her onto her back across his bed and entered her again. He fucked her furiously, with at least ten boys standing around them and a mass of others lining up behind them trying to get a good view, all of them breathing hard and shifting restlessly with every groan she made.

And then she was coming again and found herself begging, with Darren's name on her lips, to be allowed to show them something more, anything they wanted. Which is how Miss Smith found herself lying facedown on that school bed as the first of the fifty boys, at Darren's instruction, dropped his pyjama bottoms and spread her cheeks to take his turn.

Boxing Clever

Sarah Thomas was a boxer. At the age of twenty, with glorious long blonde hair and a pair of breasts you could park a mini on, you would have taken her for a model or a dancer, but the truth was that her profession was beating other young women up - all her female colleagues in the boxing game, that is. A lithe and limber lioness, she took on all challengers at the gym, her head hidden inside a padded helmet, her strong but slender body gleaming with perspiration as she spun and jabbed and hit. At the end of her third consecutive year in the amateur league, Sarah was getting ready to fight her first professional match for a major purse, and she was to fight a man. It happened like this...

Sarah's new gym, which she joined as she moved up in the ring, was attended mostly by men. This was not unusual. With the exception of the first youth club where she learned to box, and the girls had their own allotted nights to themselves, all the gyms she ever trained in were mostly full of men. Joining was not difficult, as most facilities came equipped with a girls' loo somewhere on the premises, and that was where she changed into her workout clothes in comfortable privacy. Her post-workout shower was more of a problem. The men didn't like it if she accidentally caught a glimpse of their limp cocks when she entered after a shouted warning, and they especially resented having to let her have the shower room all to herself. If somebody tried to get a peek at her, or cop-a-feel as she walked by, she knew from experience that a professional punch in the mouth, delivered with all the force of an indignant twenty-year-old who hit fifty-pound bags for a living, usually left a bruise the size of a small cauliflower and earned her a muttered apology, after which the unfortunate sod never troubled her again.

As for the looks she got, frankly, she enjoyed those. There was power in being the only girl wrapped in a towel, or dressed in skimpy shorts and a vest, walking through a gym full of sweating men reeking of testosterone. There was power in knowing that not one of them would have the nerve to raise a hand, let alone a penis, in her direction, not after the first one who tried got a black eye for his trouble.

Of course, they didn't like her. They glanced at her toned assets as she showered, and then skittered back all wet and clean and smelling of perfumed soap, to the ladies' bathroom to dress, with a mixture of irritation and barely controlled lust.

Looking back, it was only a matter of time before she ran into someone like Robbie Carlton. He was a champion in decline, but a champion nonetheless. She vaguely remembered some fight she had seen him in on television when she was a girl, during the upward swing of his career, where he'd beaten some poor skinny rival within an inch of his life. All by the rules, of course; if they don't quit, they have to be hit until they fall down. She had never followed his career, as such, but she remembered him well enough to recognise his face when she entered the new gym she was promoted to when she left the amateurs and moved to London. He had a streak of grey in his sideburns that gave the impression a flame had singed his tight curls, and there were faint bags under his eyes, but his body was as firm and muscled as it had been when he was twenty, and she recognised the look in his eyes immediately.

They were the weary eyes of someone who has killed people in the ring.

She saw him when she was sauntering through the gym in her vest and shorts for the first time. He looked up from lacing his boots when an uncanny silence fell over the large room as nearly all the men fighting and exercising stopped what they were doing to watch her. She nodded at him, and he said in a loud voice, 'What will they let in here next, bloody boxing cats?'

There was a roar of derisive male laughter, and she bit her lip.

Later, in the shower, she took her time washing her hair, and no one bothered her. For once she didn't have to hit anyone to secure her privacy. On her way to the ladies' room wrapped in her towel, she saw that most of the men were still out on the floor, including Robbie Carlton, who was busy taping up his hands. She paused for a moment, a few feet away from him where he stood at his locker, and then she slowly walked right by him.

Water dripped from her bare thighs, and her breasts were swelling dangerously out of the towel she had wrapped tightly around herself, so that only her hands holding it up covered the rosy half-moons of her nipples. 'At least the cat can still bite,' she said loudly enough for everyone to hear. 'At least the cat can still move.'

There was a shocked intake of breath all around as Carlton looked up from taping his hand at her lovely and determined face. His copper-coloured eyes stared right through her and sent a hot thrill down her spine that sparked a debilitating warmth in her pussy, which tightened deliciously as his mouth hardened angrily. Then it was war.

Two days later she found a note in her letterbox from the gym membership board. Her request for guest membership was denied. Her fee would be returned to her by cheque under separate cover the following week. *Other members have complained*, the letter said. *Significant and important voices in the club raised fierce objections to your presence.*

When she walked back out into the gym that afternoon, Robbie was there, standing amongst a group of men, and this time he was in the process of pulling off his shirt. He was some six feet tall and built of steel. She walked right up to him in her short skirt, high-heels and low-cut blouse, and she felt strangely naked when he looked her straight in the eye. She thrust the note towards him. 'Are *you* the significant voice?' she demanded.

He folded his shirt very neatly before he looked at her again. 'Girls can't box very well,' he replied. 'In fact, they're no good at it.'

'Oh, really, what *are* we good at?' she snapped, balling her hands into fists and crumpling the offending note in the process.

'Fucking, sometimes,' he replied in a husky, insulting voice, 'although in your case I might make an exception.'

'You...!' but she couldn't think of a scathing enough insult to hurl at him. She wanted to beat her fists against his rock-hard chest and smash his arrogant nose. '*You* couldn't beat a girl!' she said finally. 'You couldn't hit your way through the little silver handbag I take dancing!'

'Why should I? I don't need a fist to put you down, love. You need another part of me altogether.'

The men gathered around him laughed.

Sarah blushed red as she furiously raised a fist.

'Be careful with that,' he said, smiling, 'you might hit something.'

'I'll beat you!' she challenged. 'Five rounds. Any purse you like!' She didn't have the money, but she didn't care.

A sober silence descended on the amused crowd. Betting on a fight was illegal, and cross-gender boxing was not permitted, even privately, in a federation gym.

'I'd have to have something other than money,' Carlton said quietly.

'If you want me to leave, you have to box me,' she insisted, 'and I'll give you any prize you want if you win.'

A few men laughed appreciatively at her promise as Robbie Carlton put down his shirt and reached out to caress one of her cheeks with a large hand.

She flinched away from him automatically, and then her blush deepened as she heard him accepting her challenge. Even more furious now, she dashed out of the gym to the ladies' room to change followed by the men's humiliating laughter.

The purse, it was decided, would be five-thousand pounds; a figure arrived at when each of the men present pledged a hundred pounds to fill the pot. Sarah said she would cover it when she stood in her vest and shorts, her breasts hanging free inside the baggy top, not taped up as they would be if she had come prepared for a match with another woman. She had thrown shadow-punches at the wall and done knee bends in the loo, glancing at herself in the mirror. The shorts hugged her bottom as she bent and straightened, bent and straightened, and despite herself, she found herself admiring how good she looked in her skimpy fighting outfit. Then she entered the gym determined to knock this guy down. He would lust after her when he saw her, he would long to be inside her shorts, and it made her happy knowing he wanted to fuck her. It would make putting him away even more of a pleasure.

She stood in the ring with men all around her. They had locked the front door of the gym to keep anyone from entering during the illegal contest. She felt all their eyes on her body, on her breasts, round and firm inside her vest but jiggling softly as she stepped this way and that to warm up. She felt the deepening waves of lust flowing through the ropes protecting her. Then Rob walked into the gym, his chest gleaming with sweat, indicating he had warmed up in the changing room.

It pleased her to see that he at least took her seriously, and a cry went up from the men as he climbed into the ring with her.

He was looking at her breasts as the first bell sounded, and he came slowly towards her in the classic stance, arms bent, fists held up in front of his face. His eyes, cold and appraising, lingered on her bosom before finally settling on her face. Then he said, loudly enough for everyone to hear, 'Why don't you take that vest off, girl?'

46

She hit a right and he wasn't expecting it; her glove connected with the left side of his jaw like a brick. He flinched slightly, but then shook her blow off as easily as a cold drop of rain and came back at her with a left. She ducked and dodged him, which led her smack into the upper-cut of his powerful right.

His first punch stunned her; she had never been hit with such force before. Women simply did not have the weight of a six-foot tall, middle-weight man of forty. She found her vision swimming, and half her face went numb for a few seconds.

'Kiss that away?' he offered, dancing around her as she tried backing away from him. She took care not to stay still long enough for him to hit her again.

They danced for what felt like hours. It was merely minutes, but the music of the groaning canvas, of the men murmuring amongst themselves, the hiss of leather just missing as he swung and she ducked, the smack as she got him in the side, the stomach, the ears and the head, made it all seem to last for days. She kept hitting him in the stomach when his guard was up, and finally she landed a good one on his chin. She got him good right beneath the jaw, and he went down like a ten-ton sack of potatoes.

There was a collective gasp as he lay there at her feet like a beached whale. She stood her ground, one of his gloves resting near her ankles. There was no referee, no one to stop the fight. She would hit him until he stopped getting up!

He whispered something and she lowered her head, trying to make out what he was saying. Finally, she sank down on one knee beside him.

'I can see up your shorts,' he said. 'I like a natural blonde.'

Despite everything she felt herself smiling deep inside, and she realised she liked him looking at her pussy. She sprang to her feet again as if a snake had bitten her. 'Get him on his feet!' she demanded. 'If he can't fight, he doesn't belong in here!'

Robbie pushed himself up onto one knee, and then rose slowly, smiling at her a little groggily, but he was steady on his feet. The bastard had been fooling her.

She wound her fist up for a bigger punch, and when he caught her instead it came as a total shock. A brush to the left with his low right, which she had easily dodged, turned out to be a set-up for his left hook. He caught her square on the jaw and sent her sprawling onto her back. When she opened her eyes a moment later she saw him looming over her as she struggled to clear her head. She could see up *his* shorts now. His cock was huge, and more than just a little hard. She could see its head reddening as it stared down at her, and thought *he wants to fuck me! He wants to fuck me after he beats me*! And she was glad. Then she felt her eyes closing again...

A splash of cold water immediately brought her round. All the men were still there; she couldn't have been out more than a minute or two. She felt her nipples sticking up like pine cones against her wet T-shirt and felt as good as naked. Robbie was still standing over her, and his prick was noticeably harder. He also didn't seem to mind that she was peering up at it.

'You said *any* prize,' he reminded her. 'Take off your vest.'

She let the full implication of his request sink in before she asked, 'Here?'

'Any prize,' he repeated, 'means any place. Take it off.'

Sarah began to sit up with the intention of making a run for it, but he put one boot gently against her shoulder and pushed her back down. 'Don't bother getting up off your back,' he said, 'just raise your arms.'

Blushing as fiercely as she ever had in her life, Sarah lifted her arms so Robbie Carlton could pull her vest off and expose her breasts to all the men gathered around the ring just inches from her bared flesh.

'And now the shorts,' he said.

'Do I have to?' she asked, but she knew the answer as he slapped his gloves together impatiently. She didn't even try getting up again. Instead she rolled over, rose to her knees, and quickly shoved her shorts down as her head spun from the sudden movement and forced her to lean forward on her arms. To her horror, this position thrust her bare bottom up towards her opponent as she knelt on all fours between his feet. And there she stayed, with her shorts around her knees in a gym full of men in the middle of a boxing ring, her forehead down on the deck waiting for Robbie Carlton to do whatever he wanted to her.

There was a murmur of anticipation from the men. 'Come on, Robbie,' one of them urged, 'get stuck in and fuck her brains out!'

'Don't you boys know anything about preparation?' his deep voice growled, and then she heard the hiss of laces as he untied his boxing gloves and pulled them off. Then he rested one of his bare hands on her bottom. 'Do you admit you were wrong?' he asked her evenly.

'I'm sorry,' she breathed, aching to be fully conquered by him.

'What will you give to make it up to me?'

'I... I'm showing you everything now,' she whispered. 'What more do you want?'

'Pull your cheeks apart for me,' he said harshly.

'What?!'

'Pull your cheeks apart.'

She had expected him to shame her, but not like this; this was too humiliating by far. Biting her lip, she reached behind her with gloved hands, and struggled to pull open the cheeks of her bottom. She could almost literally feel the eyes of all the men standing around the ring on her intimate little rosebud, and also on the soft, wet lips of her pussy, puffed and hungry for Robbie, visible through the gap between her slim thighs.

'That's nice,' Robbie said, 'now beg me to fuck your arse.'

'I'm sorry?!' she gasped.

'Beg me to fuck your arse. You said I could have anything.'

'No, I'm sorry I challenged you!' she sobbed. 'I'm sorry!'

'Beg,' he insisted.

'Go on then - fuck my arse,' she cried. 'Fuck me!'

'What do you think, lads?' Robbie asked, his hands casually caressing and squeezing her firm yet yieldingly soft buttocks.

'You should oblige the little one,' one of the men answered.

'Well, maybe I will,' Robbie agreed, 'but I don't think she deserves that yet.

She wants it too much. Maybe a little smack or two on her other cheeks will make her see some sense.' And to the great delight of the assembled fighters, and to Sarah's disbelief and mortification, Robbie Carlton began spanking her with resounding smacks. A murmur of appreciation rose up from the men as his great palm made contact with her bottom, making her cheeks quiver and burn with a pain that sent sweet hot flashes of desire through her pussy. She wriggled her bottom provocatively, not caring any more who saw it. She didn't care how he fucked her now, she just wanted him to fuck her, and fuck her hard.

He spanked her for a full fifteen minutes as the men counted his blows in one great loud voice. 'Twenty-seven! Twenty-eight...! Go on, make it the thirty, Rob!' And then - Sarah wasn't sure if she was relieved or disappointed - he pulled her to her feet, lifted her out of the ring, and pushed her ahead of him into the relative privacy of the changing room.

'A man's got to have peace and quiet to do his best work, lads,' he called out, and they groaned their disappointment but did not dare follow.

And in the quiet cool of the changing room, Sarah sank to her knees again before the powerful form of Robbie Carlton as he pulled his shorts down, and his erection sprang straight out into her eager mouth. She nearly choked on his cock it was so big, but he slowly fed it to her as she struggled to take it all the way down into her throat to accommodate him, to let him go as deep as he wanted to. Then she released it and turned around, and kneeling on all fours again, offered him the soft, taut cheeks of her buttocks.

'Do you still want to?' she asked throatily. 'Do you still want to fuck my arse? I'll let you do whatever you want! You can have me however you want me!' And Robbie Carlton, champion of her youth and of her own making, promptly began pushing his long, thick dick into her bottom.

He fucked her and fucked her, thrusting and pumping his relentless erection into her tight rear passage, until she came with a scream that could easily be heard by the men ranked outside the changing room door chanting, 'Champion! Champion! Champion!'

A Short Term Let

Vanessa was an estate agent's assistant whose body was her chief asset. She had full breasts that made one want to throw her onto her back to watch them spread, and her buttocks were so delightful that heads turned all the way up and down the street whenever she went to show a property. And at the moment, those gorgeous breasts were swaying gently back and forth as she leaned over her boss' face, estate agent Martin Croupe. His mouth was suckling her hard nipples and making her moan as she rode up and down on his cock, lodged deep inside her succulent sex.

'Not bad,' he said as she lifted herself off him, holding the cigarette he had lit and then passed from his lips to hers. She lay down on her back, and watched with some interest as her large brown aureoles sank back down into the creamy round spheres of her breasts. He traced a finger beneath her high cheekbone, and gently wrapped her hair behind her ear. 'You're getting better as a lay,' he went on, 'but you're still thick as shit when it comes to selling houses.' He got out of bed and started pulling on his suit trousers.

She coughed, 'What?' choking on a mouthful of smoke. Suddenly she felt compelled to cover her breasts and pulled the sheet up over them.

'I'm sorry, love.' He reached down, plucked the cigarette out from between her fingers, and took a drag. 'You're just not working out. Nice little pussy and all, but frankly,' he looked her up and down in a way that made her feel cheap as used oil, 'the arse isn't worth what we're paying you.' And with that, he turned away and slipped on his jacket.

'But Martin,' wrapping the sheet around herself, she leapt out of bed and ran after him as he headed for the door, 'I'm just... I mean, I'm just...'

'What?' He turned back to face her, his hand on the doorknob.

'I need the job,' she said desperately, tears rising into her eyes; this was so horribly unexpected.

'Yeah, well, we all need things,' he said, and turned away again.

'No, I really, really need this job, Martin!' The air in the little apartment was almost cold - the heat hadn't been turned on before he brought her here to fuck her - and despite her distress, she felt her nipples stiffening again beneath the sheet.

'How badly do you need it?' he asked, looking at her in a strange way.

She felt an anxious tightening in her tummy. 'Very badly,' she admitted, her mouth dry. She had known she shouldn't go to bed with her boss, but she had been afraid he would sack her if she didn't, and she was sure that after he fucked her, he would want to keep her around...

'Go back to bed,' he said.

'All right,' she replied submissively.

'I'll keep this.' He yanked the sheet off her, leaving her naked in the cold passageway. Even though he had been inside her only five minutes ago, the way he looked at her as he left made Vanessa blush.

There was a sound in the corridor just outside the bedroom where Vanessa lay. It sounded like some kind of motor, or perhaps a fan, had been switched on. She couldn't be sure because she couldn't see. She was blindfolded. And she couldn't go out to investigate the sound because she was handcuffed to the bed, face down.

Vanessa was lying bound and blindfolded and completely naked in an empty apartment up for rent. There was nothing in it except for the bed upon which she lay spread-eagled and handcuffed to the brass bedstead. The bedstead and bed were a trademark of Martin's agency. 'Give them the feeling they can fuck there,' he always said, 'and they'll pay twice the going market rent.' Which was why Vanessa was not surprised to find the bed in the apartment when he first took her there, or to find herself energetically fucking him on it a few minutes later. Now, however, she did wonder where he had got to, and why. Before he

50

left, slamming the door behind him, he had turned on the heat, because it was warmer in the room. She pulled against her bonds. Why would he want the place warm now *after* he had fucked her? Yet she could not really concentrate on the question, because being tied up made her horny as sin and all she wanted was for him to come back and fuck her again.

She heard the front door open; a lock disengaged, and footsteps sounded down the hall.

'Martin?' she called, but there was only silence.

'Don't be a sod!' she cried. 'Say something!'

'The south exposure is quite grand,' she finally heard his voice commenting as he approached the bedroom and opened the door, which creaked slightly on its hinges. And then she heard the soft, gentle scuffing of another set of footsteps. Or was it two more sets? 'You'll find, gentlemen, that this flat offers opportunities most apartments do not.'

Yes, there were two more sets of footsteps! Vanessa blushed like a peach in late summer when she realised he had men with him, *two* men! She was sure of it now; she could smell aftershave that definitely wasn't his.

'Very nice, isn't it?' Martin's voice continued pleasantly. She could feel him standing over her now, which meant he could see right up into her body. She writhed against the mattress and pulled desperately on the ropes holding her legs open. There were two other men with him, and for all she knew, they were standing on either side of him enjoying an unimpeded view of her most intimate places. And suddenly, she felt a hand trace the lines of one of her shapely buttocks.

'Oh,' she gasped. 'Martin, you bastard, cover me up.'

The hand came down hard on her bottom with a ringing smack that sounded incredibly loud in the empty room.

'Ouch!' she exclaimed, more in surprise than in pain.

'The fittings and fixtures are most flexible,' Martin went on as though he couldn't hear her. Maddeningly, he was giving his usual pitch even as she felt a hand creeping up between her thighs again. She had no way of knowing if it was his hand, but she didn't want him to spank her again, so even though she writhed against the bed and pulled on her bonds, she didn't say anything as he kept on selling. 'You'll find all the original decorations, no renovations have been necessary.' The hand had reached her buttocks and was massaging one of her cheeks, making her yelp it squeezed so hard. Then she felt it rise off her before it came down again even harder.

'Oh, my God!' she gasped. 'What was that for?'

'Offer yourself up, bitch,' Martin addressed her suddenly. 'Don't you want to sell? Push your arse up.'

'Are you crazy? I'm not...'

'Push your arse up or I'll fuck you right here in front of these two gentlemen, and then you *still* won't have a job.'

Gritting her teeth, Vanessa found herself pushing her bottom up towards the punishing hand. At least she knew it was his hand now. But for how long? He

51

had just told her there were two other men in the room, she just didn't know where they were standing, or what they were thinking.

'Does she do tricks?' a deep, foreign voice inquired. She tried, but she couldn't place the accent.

'Sure, anything you like,' Martin replied.

'Now, wait a minute!' she shrieked. 'I'm not...'

'Shut up and open your mouth,' Martin commanded.

'Now wait just a minute!' she tried desperately.

'Keep your mouth nice and wide open, Vanessa. This is a sales job, remember.'

'I'm not a bloody tart! I...!' She cried out in real pain this time as something thin and flat and hard cut into her buttocks with a hiss and a crack. A riding crop? It struck her again, but this time her scream was cut off as her mouth was filled with a stiff penis. She choked a little as its owner drove it into the back of her throat and started fucking her, moving back and forth between her lips while her head was held in place by his fingers gripping her hair. She started to feel light-headed as the cock used her face like a pussy and fucked and fucked and fucked her mouth until it finally exploded, and forced her to swallow mouthful after mouthful of hot sperm surging from the balls of some strange man she couldn't even see.

Vanessa gasped for air when the blindfold was pulled off, and she lay panting on the bed after the thankfully spent erection slipped out of her mouth. The light hurt her eyes at first, then her blurred vision focused, and glancing over her shoulder, she saw Martin standing in his coat just behind her. To her right, a man in a beige suit was zipping up his fly. Another man, wearing a grey charcoal morning coat, was standing beside Martin directly behind her - right between her open legs - and he was holding a small vial. Both the strangers were black, a very deep black like ebony. She blinked in an effort to clear her head as she looked back at Martin again. 'You bastard,' she hissed.

'Don't worry, sweetie, you're not finished yet,' he said condescendingly, nodded, and the man in the coat approached the bed as he opened the vial in his hand.

'No, Martin, no,' she panted. 'I'm not...'

'Do you want a job?' he asked in a maddeningly reasonable tone.

'No, I don't...' she spat, before adding, 'what's he doing?'

The man in the morning coat squeezed some white liquid onto his palm as he knelt between her legs at the end of the mattress. She felt his fingers slip between the cheeks of her bottom, and then one of them slipped into her anus and very efficiently lubricated her tight back passage with the cool, greasy ointment.

'No,' she murmured. 'Martin, don't let him do this to me. I'm not...'

'*What* aren't you?' He had lit a cigarette and was leaning back against the wall, watching as the man finished greasing her rear hole, knelt up, and began undoing his trousers.

'I'm not for sale,' Vanessa sobbed into the pillow. 'I'm not for sale...'

'But it looks to me like you can be rented,' Martin said.

She shook her head as the second man, now free of his trousers and boxer shorts, crawled towards her on the bed, his long brown cock fully erect. He spread himself on top of her, and gently kissed the soft curls at the nape of her neck as his heavy body pressed her down into the mattress. Then he reached down to part her cheeks, and began thrusting his penis slowly, insistently and inexorably into her bottom...

As she lay quietly, her flushed cheek on the pillow, Martin came back into the room holding the contract he had just signed with the two clients before they left, along with a cheque. He waved it back and forth in her face. 'Maybe you have a future in this business after all,' he said, sitting down beside her on the bed.

'That was terrible,' she said flatly. 'Terrible.'

'What was terrible?' he mocked. 'The fact that they were foreigners? That your arse is too tight?'

'I'm not a whore,' she complained. 'I'm a professional woman. I can do the job. I can sell. You didn't have to let them have my body.'

'Well, sweetie,' Martin pulled his tie loose, 'it's like this. I didn't really let them have your body, I simply renegotiated the fixtures. You want to sell, don't you?'

'What do you mean?'

He undid the top button of his shirt. 'You're the agent of record on this letting. The commission is yours. You'll be collecting, of course.' He kicked off his shoes.

'I get commission?'

'Yes, you're the commission agent. You get all the money. But you have to come and collect it every month from them.' He took off his jacket.

'You mean, I'll have to...?'

'I expect you will, my dear, I expect you will. Still, it's a nice big letting, and I'm sure you want to keep your job.' He took off his trousers.

'You expect to fuck me again now?' she whispered. 'You treat me like a whore, and then you want to fuck me again? Let me up. Please, untie me. Let me up.'

'Can't do that.' He folded his trousers neatly, and hung them over the brass bedstead.

'Let me up,' she cried.

'No. You see, the cheque hasn't cleared yet, so I can't be sure they'll honour the contract. A letting isn't a letting until the money clears, I'm sure you'll agree. So, I have to show the property again in half an hour.'

Vanessa's eyes widened in disbelief. 'You mean...?'

'Yes, two Japanese gentlemen. Lovely chaps. Well, they sounded lovely on the phone. Anyway, they haven't got anything you haven't had before, an old professional like you. You do whatever it takes to get the job done, don't you?'

She felt the blood rushing to her face again, and suddenly she suffered the impression that she would be tied to that bed for the rest of her life.

'Aren't you a professional, Vanessa?'

'I just wanted to keep my job,' she said in a small voice.

'Didn't you sleep with me to keep the job?'

'Maybe...'

'Well, do it once, and you may as well do it a thousand times. Which you may very well have to, if you want to keep working for me. A lot of beds in a lot of short-term lets. But the money's good. You can't really sell your arse more than once, my love. Only once, over and over, a thousand times. A million times. But it's a lovely pair of cheeks you have, and I'm sure you'll love the closings. Speaking of which, we only have twenty minutes, so push your bum up for me. Can't very well have the clients getting better service from my staff than I get myself.'

Vanessa felt her tears dry on her face as he kissed the back of her neck like the second man had done. She turned her face to look at him, and found his cock next to her mouth. She knew she had to suck it, and she did, until he pulled it out of her mouth, slick with her saliva, and thrust it without any further lubrication into her bottom, and she begged him to go slowly.

'All right, anything Vanessa wants,' he whispered into her ear, and ploughed his erection into her from behind over and over again. Yet she still found herself writhing against the mattress in the throes of a blinding climax as he penetrated her deeply and inescapably, and she listened for footsteps on the stairway outside announcing more clients coming to rent her body.

Blowing Your Aces

My husband likes me to play cards with his friends. He likes me to play strip poker with his friends. It all began quite innocently. The game was a regular event. The guys would drop by the house on Thursday or Friday night and play a few hands, just my husband and three of his bowling buddies - Frank, Eddie and Mike. My husband, Billy, is a sociable guy, he likes hanging out with the boys, and who was I to object if he brought them home once a week; at least it meant he was home.

One night I was bringing them some snacks - little frankfurters on sticks and potato chips and dip - like I usually did, it was only hospitable. Billy used to like showing me off to his buddies before we got married, so I thought the least I could do was help him out when he entertained them. I wore a short dress every now and then, I won't deny it. Hell, I'm entitled to a little excitement, same as the next girl.

Well, on this particular night, Billy was losing badly. He loved playing cards but they never seemed to like him, especially the aces, if you know what I mean. He was holding on to nothing while Frank seemed to be picking up all the good cards. Frank had always liked me, and his eyes lingered openly on me when I was in the room. Frank had money; whenever we went out as a gang, Frank never was short of change to buy the rounds. And he always dressed well, not like Billy's other friends. Now that he and Billy were gambling together regularly, Frank was picking up ten, twenty notes a night from him, and they were notes my dear husband couldn't afford.

On the night I'm talking about, as I was bringing in the tray of frankfurters, Bill was cursing the latest of his worthless hands. Meanwhile, smiling in satisfaction at his own spread, Frank gave me a long, leisurely look, his eyes lingering on my cleavage - well-displayed by my tight black sweater's deep V-neck - as I bent to kiss Billy's neck. I was wearing a matching short black skirt and black pantyhose with high-heels, and I deliberately hadn't bothered with a bra.

'Bill, how about I cut you a break on those expensive hands you keep playing?' Frank offered as he reached over and speared a frankfurter off the tray from directly beneath my bosom.

'What you talking about, Frank?' Billy sounded tired, and he barely seemed to notice when I kissed him. He was studying his cards and rubbing his face.

'Well, how about we widen the betting frame?' Frank's voice sounded strangely dreamy, distant, dangerous. I don't know why, but that's the feeling I got when I looked at his inscrutable smile.

'What terms?' Bill asked, throwing out a card. It was the wrong one, even I could have told him that, but he never listens to me. He glanced up at Frank, wiping sweat off his brow. The other two men were listening intently, which in retrospect leads me to suspect they had talked this out between them beforehand.

'Well,' Frank went on, 'the way I see it, you're down fifteen-hundred already tonight. That makes nearly five-thousand you've dropped this month, and it's only the third game of the month. You got that kind of money, Billy?'

'Don't worry about my kind of money,' my husband said, slipping his arm around my waist and resting his hand on my bottom. He always did that whenever his manhood was challenged.

'Well, don't you have any other kind of assets you could show?' Frank riffled his cards gently with one hand.

'Like what?' Billy sounded curious now.

'Like what your hand's on,' Frank replied, his smile deepening. Mike chuckled, and Eddie cleared his throat as he shifted a little in his chair. The three of them had talked it over beforehand, I'm sure of it. I wore short skirts around them, yes, but I hadn't asked for this. Billy will tell you I never asked for this. At the time I wasn't exactly sure for a moment what Frank meant, but Billy knew straight off. I saw a blush creeping up his neck and looked at him in surprise. I had just grasped what Frank was implying and had been about to laugh it off until I saw Billy, my Billy, blushing. Why should he be blushing unless he'd had some thoughts along these lines himself? I was beside myself when I suddenly realised my husband had considered betting me in poker, but before I could react, I heard him ask, 'You thinking a hundred dollars a garment?'

'Well,' Frank said, 'a garment per pot, or if it gets bigger, I guess a garment for every hundred dollars, sure. You guys interested enough in seeing Fanny's goods to spot Bill a hundred a garment, boys?'

Eddie and Mike both grunted in agreement, careful not to look at me.

'Now wait a goddamned minute,' I said, slapping Billy's hand off me. 'You're not talking about me like I'm not in the goddamned room, are you? This is *my* parlour.'

'It's an eat-in kitchen,' Billy corrected me, 'and you always say we can't afford what I'm losing.'

'So stop losing!' I felt myself blushing to the roots of my hair, but I do believe the truth is that I found it all very exciting and that's why I sounded so angry. 'You don't have to keep playing, Billy.' I was aware of the fact that Frank's eyes never left my breasts, in fact, the feel of them resting on my cleavage just got warmer and warmer. I folded my arms across my chest.

'It's not quite as simple as that, Fanny.' Frank reached across the table and speared another frankfurter. 'Billy's been losing pretty regularly lately, and when I ask - that is, when Eddie, Mike and me ask - if he can afford that kind of money, we're not referring to whether or not he can afford to lose what he hasn't lost yet, it's whether he can afford to pay what he already owes.'

'You mean...?'

'Oh yes,' Frank said, biting the sausage off the toothpick and then twirling the stick around and around between his fingers. 'He owes way more than what's been going out of your account. What he's been dropping on the table in front of you is nothing. We've been gambling on Tuesday nights too, and sometimes Wednesday nights, every time he told you he was at work.'

I sat down in the empty chair beside Billy's, my head spinning. I couldn't think, but I knew I was playing this game whether I held the cards in my hand or not, and I could feel my face getting redder and warmer. Then, his eyes meeting mine, Frank laughed softly and put his cards down.

First, Billy bet a two pair and an ace against what turned out to be the straight flush in Eddie's hand, at which point I slipped off my high-heels.

'Come on,' Eddie frowned, wanted me to take more off than just my shoes, but I ignored him and Frank waved him quiet. Billy wouldn't look at me as he bet a two of diamonds next and an ace backed by a king, but Mike easily beat that, and my skirt came off. I was still wearing more than I would normally wear at the beach, except that they had me get up on a chair to strip. With my back to them, I pulled my skirt up my thighs, unzipped it, and stepped out of it while thrusting my bottom over the table for all of them to see. I was glad I was wearing pantyhose and not the garter-belt Billy normally likes me to wear. The way I see it, they were getting enough for their money, I didn't need to provide any extras.

I was starting to tear up a little, and I sniffled as I sat back down. I knew what was coming off next, and Billy still wouldn't look at me. His friends were definitely looking though, looking hard and smiling smugly.

Then my husband lost again. I forget what cards he played, and I wouldn't look at anyone, just sat in my chair and swallowed. Finally I grasped the hem of my sweater with both hands and slid forward as far as I could in an effort to hide behind the table as I pulled the black folds up to just below my chest, and took a deep breath. The men were staring at my belly, what they could see of it over the table, and piling up their money. I closed my eyes, and pulled the sweater up over my face. I could feel their stares warming up the cool air as it hit my naked breasts, which swayed enticingly as they came free of the tight sweater. My nipples were getting stiff, and I wasn't sure if it was because it was chilly in the room or if it was because I could seem to feel all their hot breaths on them. I kept the sweater over my face like a veil as I felt their lust like the ghost of a caress on my flesh that made he shiver.

'Let's see your face, too,' I heard Frank say through the soft cotton folds. 'We get that for free.'

I blinked against the light from the lamp as I pulled my sweater off all the way, and sat topless before them. Then there came the last hand, or the next to last hand. Mike and Eddie had both folded by then, so it was just Frank and Billy. My husband drew a card, then another one, and another one as Frank just kept smiling. He didn't care about the money. He kept putting out another card, and winking at me as he turned his eyes down towards the table as if he could see through it. He called, finally, the last card was revealed, and Billy lost just like I knew he would. Yet I knew he had been fighting to salvage the last shreds of my dignity. I think he had liked the idea of my getting naked in front of his friends much more than the actual event. But now he had lost, and I had to strip completely.

'Come on, honey,' Frank said softly, 'don't be shy. Come out from behind the table.'

'And what if I don't?' I asked defiantly.

'What do you mean?' Billy beat Frank to the question, eagerly hoping I could find a way out of this for us.

'What if you play another hand?' I asked.

'What else you got to offer?' Frank's smile never wavered.

'I wouldn't get up from behind this table,' I said.

'You've *got* to get up,' Billy said, looking worried.

'I don't have to get up from behind this table,' I said, clenching my hands in my lap. 'I won't get up from it and take my panties off for you three lechers, but...' I looked into Frank's eyes. 'I could get down under it...'

'What are you talking about?' My husband looked pale.

Frank's smile vanished as his stare became penetratingly intense.

'Another hand,' I said, 'and you better win, Billy, because I'm going to get under this table and blow whoever wins the next hand. Double or quits for the money, Frank.'

Frank nodded. Billy had his head in his hands. I sank down even further in my chair and tried to make like I was as brave as I sounded. I just knew I wasn't about to show my bare bottom to the four of them in my own parlour.

The cards fell again. I don't suppose you have a hard time imagining how Billy played. He bet an even stupider hand than usual against Frank's brilliant hand. I suspect Frank cheats, but that doesn't count for much when it comes time to collect.

Billy crushed his cards when he lost. Why it came as such a surprise to him, or to me for that matter, I don't know, but the fact is it shocked us seeing all those aces lying in front of Frank like goal posts. There was no doubt about the fact that I was going to have to crawl over there now and make him happy.

Mike and Eddie refused to leave, and Billy said he had a right to watch, and I was too shocked to argue. I slipped under the table, and I could see all their heads peering down at me as I crawled on all fours across the floor to Frank's knees. His hard-on was enormous inside his black slacks, which made unzipping them difficult as his bulge pressed up against his fly. To my left, Billy's moon-like face was panting in distress, and in the darkness beneath the table, I detected the starry glimmer of tears on his cheeks. My own eyes were completely dry as I wet my lips.

'That's it, baby,' Frank said. He was the only one not looking down at me, the only one who didn't seem interested in watching me do this thing.

I reached into his slacks and eased his cock gently out of his fly, careful not to let it brush his zipper's jagged metal teeth. His head was a hot purple, and his thick shaft was deep red all the way down. I grasped it gently in my hand as it thrust rigidly out at me.

'That's it now, baby,' I heard him say through the table. 'I've dreamed of you doing this. Now, put me in your mouth.'

I licked him with the tip of my tongue. He tasted salty, he tasted of pre-cum and salt, and I liked his flavour. I slipped my lips over his head, and he bucked up to meet me. Slipping lower in his chair, he cradled my neck in one hand and pushed down on the back of my head. I leaned down to swallow him more deeply, and he pushed my face into his lap and thrust himself into my throat. His fingers in my hair, he moved my head up and down slowly at first, and then fast and faster until he suddenly held me hard against him and made me swallow while he pumped and pumped and pumped his pleasure down my throat and I nearly choked. I closed my eyes but I could still hear Mike and Eddie laughing as they watched me blow their buddy, and watched Bill watching his wife going down on another man right in front of him.

Billy was the one who insisted on spanking me for the family honour, but it was really just to make himself feel better. I guess he had to prove he was still a man. He said I had to be punished for being unfaithful.

'If I should be punished for being unfaithful,' I retorted, 'then what should you be for losing all that money in the first place?'

Of course, he didn't see it that way. He had me stick my bottom out over one end of the table and suffer stinging licks from his thin leather belt. I had bought him that belt when we were first married, and it hurt like hell to have it kissing my skin even through my hose and panties. I cried out so loudly after the third lash that he stopped, saying maybe I had learned my lesson already. The three other men clearly enjoyed watching me being beaten. Frank asked Billy how much he would charge to let each one of them take a belt to me, and my husband punched him in the mouth.

Well, after that it was all natural enough, in a way. After Frank beat Billy up, things got settled. First, Eddie told Billy what he owed him personally, and then Mike explained how he had notes going back for years. So I was forced to take them off. Yes, I took my panties off, finally, but I did it under the table. I lay back and eased my white lace panties down my legs along with my black pantyhose while they all looked down at me. Then Eddie felt me between my legs, kissed me on the lips, and fucked me. I closed my eyes and crossed my knees over his back as he rode me, diving deep into my pussy, and Billy cried and hid his face in his hands.

Then, of course, there was that little matter of Mike's tab. Billy owed him more money than anyone, so I agreed to his demands. Billy went and got a pillow, and I buried my face in it while Mike fucked my tight little bottom. He greased me up with some butter first, and then slid into me slowly, almost tenderly. And when he came in my rear passage, he kissed the back of my neck and said, 'Thanks, sweetheart.' That's more than Billy ever did when he took me from behind like that.

Which brings me back to Billy. He doesn't fuck me any more, he says he can't. Which is why I guess he likes his friends to play cards with me, in the sense that they play for my bottom, my pussy, my mouth, and my breasts. No, Billy doesn't fuck me any more, which is why, I suppose, he loves it when his friends come by every Thursday and Friday night and he can watch me where I sit under the table sucking their cocks, one after the other.

The Second Hand

Anna worked on the high street where the second-hand shops and charity stores blended in with the fine boutiques. Her breasts were lovely and generous, and men would stop as they passed the dress boutique where she worked and stare at her. Yet she scarcely seemed to notice them as she stood on the opposite side of the usually rain-streaked glass hoping for something better in life. She was tired of just standing in a dress shop wearing tight-fitting black clothes, with her blonde hair pinned up in a cute little bun to make her neck look even longer than it was and to enhance the fullness of her breasts. The management liked her large bosom because it attracted customers, mainly men out buying a gift for their wives or girlfriends and indulging themselves in the process. They would walk in off the street, and looking a little embarrassed would ask her if she could help them pick something out for someone special.

'What size is she?' she would ask professionally.

And they would invariably reply, 'Oh, just about your size.'

She would then say, 'Follow me,' while thinking, *In your dreams*!

On this particular day, Anna was pining away as usual. She was standing at the window, tugging her black sweater down to smooth out her shapely silhouette in the tight black dress, when the old fool who ran the charity shop across the street, *Second Hands*, wove his way through the busy traffic and entered the store. He was about six-feet tall and dressed in a chequered shirt that smelled faintly of damp and mildew.

'Can I help you?' Anna asked a bit dismissively. She had occasionally caught him looking out at her, and she had not liked the way he focused on her breasts.

'I've come to see the manager about a little problem,' the old man wheezed slightly as he spoke. 'There's a little something he might want to know about. Well, he might not *want* to know about it, but then again, he might. Know what I mean?' He winked at her.

'I'm sure I don't,' Anna replied. 'In any event, you can talk to me. The manager won't be in until later today, and maybe not until tomorrow.'

'You authorised?' He may once have been handsome, but years of hard living had taken their toll. The smell of damp clothing hung around him like old smoke.

'I run the shop,' Anna said briskly. 'What can I do for you?' She was hoping a client would come in and force this conversation to a swift conclusion.

'We've been getting your coats,' the old man said. His eyes twinkled as he eyed her up and down, beginning with her feet in black high-heels and ending with her golden hair. 'We been getting your coats in our store as donations, and I don't think that lot's been paid for. Know what I mean? Come and take a look.'

She said she couldn't possibly leave the store during business hours, but she would tell the manager, and if he did not come in today, then she would go see for herself later.

'All right, suit yourself,' he said, 'but don't wait too long. I can't keep them off the shelf forever. We got homeless to cater for. All right, little one?'

'Don't call me that, please. I'll see what I can do about visiting your shop later.'

He smiled, and practically skipped back across the street.

Anna stepped into the store with its charity smell of damp old clothes and used linen. It was just gone six o'clock when her manager had arrived to count the money, and sent her off to see what this nonsense was about as he licked his thumb on piles of twenty and fifty-pound notes.

The old man was expecting her. 'In the back,' he said with a glee she found altogether too frisky. And what bothered her was that his gentlemanly mannerisms were awaking a strange Sunday afternoon movie nostalgia in her as she imagined what he must have looked like forty years ago. He must have been a handsome man, and it made her sad to see him now, so old and shrivelled. 'In the back,' he repeated, looking into her bright young eyes with his own equally bright old ones. 'I've got it all ready for you, little one.'

'If you insist,' she said wearily. 'I've got to be back across the street to see my boss in...' her breath caught in mid-sentence when she stepped into the back room. She had steeled herself for the miserable sight of racks hung with old worn-out clothes, but what she walked into instead was a veritable treasure trove. If she hadn't known better she would have thought she was back across the street. Every coat they had ever sold seemed to be here. Every dress she had ever modelled herself and gift-wrapped was here. Every dress too expensive to stock more than two or three of hung in this back room by the dozens. 'What on earth have you been doing?' she demanded breathlessly.

'Sit down,' he told her.

She felt a chair pushing against the backs of her legs. 'Thank you,' she said, as her knees gave way beneath her.

'It started with one or two.' The old man sat down and leaned towards her in a conspiratorial way, his eyebrows a shining salt-and-pepper beneath the overhead light. 'My name is Walker,' he told her, 'Pat Walker, but everybody calls me Pat because I like to pat. Know what I mean?' He smiled at her, and she felt that strangely stimulating Sunday afternoon and old movies sensation stir in her belly again. 'One day,' he went on, 'there were one or two dresses in a bag, and then a coat. Then one day, there was an entire rack!'

'No,' she gasped.

'Out back,' he said, 'under the balcony, out of the rain. Nice gear, this lot, not your usual muck.'

'We sell only the best to young women,' she explained, quickly estimating the value of this amazing back room. How could her manager not know about this?

'I know your young women,' the old man said dismissively. 'Not one of them comes here to say hello.'

'Well...' Anna shifted her legs beneath her. The skirt she was wearing today was short, and more of her thighs were exposed to his eyes than she would have liked.

He touched her arm. 'I don't mean they should give of themselves,' he said, 'just a hello. It's a cold, cruel world for the homeless, and even for those who care for them. A "hello" in the right place saves a thousand pounds of stolen goods. And a little squeeze...' He put his hand on hers. She could not believe it, but with all the naturalness in the world, as though her body belonged to him, he touched one of her breasts, resting his hand gently and appreciatively on its swelling warmth.

'I don't believe this,' Anna leapt up out of the chair. 'How dare you, you filthy old...?'

'Now, now, little one, Pat didn't mean to startle you.'

'Don't call me that!'

'That's what your granddad called you, isn't't?'

'None of your business! I'll tell my boss you've got... some merchandise of his!'

'You do that,' he said, and smiled as she fled.

Her boss, an Iranian businessman who always wore a black leather coat and was balding, had no time for this. 'Go get the coats and the dresses, all of it! It's your fault they went missing in the first place. I knew this store lost money!'

'I wasn't responsible for this!' Anna declared. 'How could I be?'

'I don't care how, you just are!' her boss barked back. 'Go get my merchandise!

You don't get the merchandise back, you got no job!' He stuck the money he had been counting in his pockets, and left. He walked past the window on his way down the pavement, and watching him go, she caught sight of the old man, Pat Walker, putting one of her store's more expensive dresses on a mannequin inside the charity shop's display window.

'I'm very sorry,' she found herself saying to Pat a few minutes later where she once again stood in the back room of his shop, 'about before.'

'About what before?' he asked cheerfully.

'The... misunderstanding.' She blushed. Despite herself, she could feel something inside her, deep down inside her, stirring for this old man, which made matters even worse. It was like being attacked from both sides, inside and out.

'Oh? I thought you said it wasn't your stock, little one.'

'Well, you see, my boss says I've got to get it back. It's our stock, all right.'

'Oh. Then what was the misunderstanding about?' He looked genuinely perplexed.

'I just... I'm sorry, I didn't... I'm sorry more young women don't stop by and say hello. I'm sorry they don't... give of themselves. It must make your job very...'

'Lonely? No, I don't think so. You know, I believe there *was* a misunderstanding. I don't think this is your stock at all, that's why I've begun putting it out. That dress in the window, lovely, isn't it?'

'Don't...'

'Don't what?'

'Nothing,' she said quickly.

'Yes, well, it's amazing what some people leave out. It's a waste, I say.'

'Please,' Anna begged softly.

'I'm sorry?'

'I have to get all the stock back,' she whispered in desperation. 'My boss will kill me if I don't. He'll...'

'He'll what?'

'It is our stock!'

'I tell you what,' Pat Walker said, 'as it's your stock, and you model it to the customers over there... that's what you do, isn't it, model?'

'I'm the manager... well, the assistant manager.'

'One of these must fit you, mustn't it? Stands to reason, doesn't it, little one? One of these must fit you, if it's your stock and you modelled it. So, why not try one of them on for me and see how it hangs?'

'You don't wear anything under dresses like these,' Anna heard herself say, and blushed suddenly, even though she wasn't sure why. 'You can't get such a fine dress to hang over a bra and panties.'

'Is that a problem?' Pat asked, his eyes twinkling. 'You don't have anything I haven't seen before, unless women have changed in the last few decades. Have women changed, little one?'

Her blush deepened; he was getting to her, this decrepit old man was actually getting to her! 'Where could I change? And it's cold...'

'You could change right here. I'll put the gas fire on for you. Just change right here, my dear. It's a cold world out there for the charitable. You don't have to have stock, we manage here without it, I'm just not sure *you* can manage, without your job, that is. Can you manage without it, little one?'

Anna sighed.

He put the gas fire on for her. Its two bars, gold and red, flickered cosily as she stood in the back room of the charity shop and handed her clothes over to him. First came her shoes, black stilettos heels shiny as coals. He took them from her, and set them down on a shelf full of stuffed bears. Then she rolled her tights down from beneath her skirt with her back to him, so as not to show him too much. But he got impatient and rested a hand on her bottom, a light, appreciative hand.

'Please, don't,' she said.

'Is it your stock, or mine?' he asked gently.

'We'll see,' her own voice sounded strangely husky to her, 'once I've tried it on.' She took her skirt off.

His eyes travelled up and down her long legs. She stood there in her panties and a bodice over her strapless bra as he laid the fine garment she was to put on over an empty dress stand. Then he waited.

Sighing again, she reached behind to snap open the bodice, and then bent forward to let it fall off her.

He took it from her. 'Now take off your bra,' he said.

'Do I have to?' she asked in the petulant tone of a little girl.

'The stock doesn't belong to anyone,' he said, 'it's what you give that gets you to heaven.'

She reached back again, and unhooked her bra. The lace cups fell away and her breasts, full and pink and standing erect in the chilly room, hung free. She gasped when his frail, dry hand immediately took hold of one of them and caressed it as gently as he had before. 'And my panties?' she whispered.

'You don't have to take those off, my dear,' he said, smiling. 'What's a gentleman for?' And he slipped his fingers into her panties, slipped them down around her thighs, and cupped her warm young mound in his cool old hand. He fumbled a bit with his fly, and she instinctively reached out to help him pull his zipper down, curious to reach inside his pants and feel his wiry white hairs.

When, on her knees before him, she had licked him erect - her tongue awakening a surprisingly big and firm prick out of all that soft, snowy hair - he made her lie back on a pile of coats beside the softly hissing gas fire. Then he spread her legs and drove his cock into her slowly. Eventually, she found herself coming as the old man kept thrusting patiently into her pussy, seemingly in no rush to come himself. She groaned as she climaxed, and afterwards he caressed her brow gently. 'Little one,' he said, 'you just don't meet the right men.'

In the morning she woke up on the creased coats covered with a blanket Pat had spread over her. And in the doorway of the charity shop's loading bay at the back of the store stood her manager handing Pat a twenty-pound note. 'It's very cheap storage, don't you think, Anna? Very cheap storage back here for stock, not expensive like it is across the street.' Her boss laughed. 'You like this old man? In my country we have a saying, "look after the old, because what you give them you will one day take for yourself". Don't forget the dress!' And he left, trailing laughter behind him.

Pat helped her up. She was still naked, and he insisted she put on the expensive garment. 'No, you earned it,' he said when she protested. 'It is your stock, little one. Don't you let it get cold.' And he kissed her until she felt that wonderful golden warmth in her pussy again.

'Do you watch old movies, little one?'

'Yes.'

'Well then, why don't you bend over this chair for me like a good girl.'

She did as he said, and he lifted the shining dress up over her lovely bottom, and took a cane to it. He used an old bamboo cane someone had donated, a swishy cane that seemed to cut right through her flesh. When he lifted the weapon up for her to see, her eyes widened in alarm, but he promised her he would be gentle. She nodded, and lowering her head, waited for the first stroke to fall.

It burned impossibly. 'Ah!' she cried.

'Only five more,' Pat said. 'You can't have less than six, it's tradition.'

'Please, just use your hand, Mr Walker,' she begged. 'I'm not as strong as women used to be. I'm...'

'Just a girl,' Pat finished for her. 'All right, little one, just my hand, but it'll have to be the full dozen then on your lovely bottom.'

She nodded, and bit her lip.

The spanks were soft, at first, and after the terrible burn of the cane, they barely hurt. He smacked her on each cheek, and then let her rest a moment. Gradually, however, her bottom began glowing as it warmed up, and by the tenth smack her cheeks were blazing like a furnace. He stopped to caress them, and to cool their heat by blowing on them.

'Two more, then a treat,' he said, and spanked her two more times before, to her amazement, he broke out a small jar of cold cream. 'Oh no, little one, good girls deserve favours.' And his fingers rubbed the wonderfully cool cream into her flaming buttocks, very slowly and gently, until the fiery discomfort dimmed and flowed down into her pussy as a deliciously exciting warmth. And then he greased her, his cunning fingers dipping down into the valley between her now cool, sleek cheeks.

His cold-cream laden finger thrust gently into her anus, and then his slim old cock slipped comfortably deep into her bottom. He penetrated her with surprising strength and speed, and glancing over her shoulder at him, she could have sworn that as he took her from behind, ramming his miraculously rampant old rod into her willing buttocks, Pat Walker looked like a young man... it was nineteen-thirty again and she was coming and coming forever...

Piano Teacher Played

Cora Brown taught piano in her tiny apartment at the top of the tower block, and the pupils who came to her - from the local school that couldn't afford to keep a full-time music teacher on staff - were mostly boys. She had taught girls once a few years ago, but now most of her students were boys, and she sometimes wondered if this had anything to do with her outfits.

She taught A-Level piano for boys sixteen to eighteen-years-old, and she wore tight dresses that hugged her breasts and tied her blonde hair back in a prim little bun that left her bosom and elegant shoulders fully exposed.

Sometimes, in the summer especially, she wore skimpy shorts. A breeze would play through the tall tower block windows she enjoyed feeling on her bare legs, and all the students who walked through her door invariably looked down at her thighs, and blushed.

Her star pupil, who was taking his exams this summer, was Paul. He was blond and thin but solidly built, he had long, angular hands ideal for a pianist, and he hated practice. Yet he played like an angel when he made the effort.

He could definitely play, she reflected as she pinned her hair up in the hall mirror just prior to his arrival. He played like a devil. But he didn't like to practice, and if he didn't practice, he would fail his exams, and that would be that.

'Do it again, Paul,' she said after he had taken a trial run at the short Grieg.

He was not wearing a school uniform; the sixth formers wear permitted to wear their own clothes to school. Personally, she liked the regulation blazers and ties.

Paul, however, was obviously much more comfortable in his blue tracksuit bottoms and grey sweatshirt, and he wasn't in the least bit interested in playing Grieg again. He was staring at her breasts, and he didn't blush when he looked up and caught her eyes on him. He simply turned his head and stared out the window at some pigeons perched on the ledge.

'Paul...' she said.

'Yes?'

'Do you want to fail?'

'What's the difference, it's all a con anyway. I'm not going to play the piano when I get out of school, I can't get a grant.'

'You can play for pleasure.'

'No pleasure in it,' he replied shortly.

She sighed. This was always the way it was with Paul. He made a show of his resistance, and then he got the piece in his head and the notes flowed like water off his fingers. But he didn't have any time to waste now. This was the exam piece, and he only had two weeks to get it right. 'There will be time for pleasure later,' she assured him.

'I can't concentrate,' he said.

'Paul, you're the best student they've got. If you fail, they might lose the funding for the music option.'

'Not my fault.' He looked bored as he snuck another glance at her breasts.

She let out a slow, patient breath, and watched his gaze follow her bosom up and down. Suddenly she was annoyed. 'Paul, I could lose my job!' she snapped. 'I could lose this flat! And then you couldn't stare at my tits any more!'

He met her eye. 'If I couldn't look at them, I wouldn't come here at all.' He smiled. He wasn't even embarrassed by what he had just said.

'Is that all you come here for?' she demanded, really angry now. And, for some reason, she was blushing. Perhaps she was a little flattered too...

'No offence, Cora... I mean, Miss Brown.'

'I try to teach you something,' she muttered, 'and what do I get for it?'

'Not my fault if there's no pleasure for me in playing.'

'What would it take to get you to practice, Paul?'

'I don't know.' He looked her up and down. 'A bit of fun, I think.'

'Looking at my breasts?' she asked, more out of desperation than anything.

'Yeah, all right.'

'What?'

'I'll practice if you show me your breasts. It's a start, isn't it?'

She laughed out loud. 'You're kidding, right?'

'I can't think of any other reason to practice,' he replied seriously.

'I could punish you if you don't!' she snapped, outraged.

'You'll punish me if I don't? How?' He smiled lazily.

'I could punish you by not letting you come back here ever again, and then you wouldn't see my breasts at all, not even through my blouse!'

He raised an eyebrow. 'And if I do practice?'

'We'll see.' She had crossed her arms over her chest during this exchange, and now the way his smile deepened made her cross her legs as well.

Unfortunately, she didn't have another student coming that afternoon, and perhaps that is why - as she told herself later - things got out of hand. That is what she told herself, anyway. Paul laid down his terms. He said he would play for an hour, and after that, she would pay up.

'Just like that?' She was almost laughing it was so outrageous to be bargaining with one of her students like this.

'You're the one who wants me to practice,' he pointed out. 'And that's just for starters.'

'Oh? What's for afters?'

'You wanted to punish me for not practising, didn't you?'

'Yes,' she answered slowly, wondering where he was going with this.

'We'll have to think of something if I play for more than an hour,' he replied. 'What's the opposite of you punishing me?'

'It's me even letting you think about seeing me topless,' she said, and rising from the seat, she left the room.

She went shopping while he practiced. She bought a new pair of panties and some fresh razors. When she returned, even before she walked through the door, she could hear the piano. He was still playing.

She went into the bathroom, shaved beneath her arms, dabbed on some perfume, and gazed at her face in the mirror. 'He's not a date,' she scolded herself out loud, 'he's an eighteen-year-old boy. He couldn't care less what you smell like, let alone if you're smooth. How would he ever know, anyway?' And she stuck her tongue out at herself. Then, with a start, she realised the hour must be up because he had stopped playing.

Almost shyly, she opened the bathroom door and walked back into the main room.

'Do you want to hear me play?' he asked. His eyes focused on her intently, as if he noticed something was different about her, and suddenly he smiled.

She blushed. 'I heard you,' she said.

'Go on then.'

'With what?' she asked innocently.

'Show me how smooth you shaved your armpits. Go on, put your arms over your head and I'll help you take off your dress.'

'How did you know I had shaved myself?' She was astonished, and excited by how perceptive he obviously was.

'Well, I didn't think you'd shaved your pussy for me Cora, not on the first date.'

His smile was maddening. 'I can't,' she said simply.

'Then I won't take the exam.'

She looked at him, at his tousled blond hair. Just a few years ago he had been a child, now he was a man waiting to take charge of something, of someone, of her.

'You're the one who's worried about your job,' he reminded her. 'I don't have a job playing the piano, you have a job teaching me.'

'What if I don't want to?' she asked softly.

'You'll do as you're told.' His voice was equally soft, but the unquestionably firm note in it thrilled her. She found herself grasping the hem of her short skirt, and she felt that unmistakable current of excitement in the pit of her stomach again. She wasn't wearing a bra, and suddenly she was tempted to pull down the low neckline of her dress and let him look at her breasts to his heart's content.

'No,' he said when he saw what she was doing, 'take it off.'

'We didn't say anything about...'

'Do you want me to play, or not?'

'This is blackmail.'

'What do you call offering to give me what I want in exchange for what you want?'

'A reasonable exchange,' she retorted.

'Then get your kit off.'

She felt her pussy getting dangerously warm as she turned her back on him, and pulled her zipper down. She shrugged her delicate shoulders, and the dress slid off her slowly. She felt the breeze wafting in through the windows caress her bare breasts, and then her bottom in the skimpy panties she was wearing. They were made of a nearly transparent silk, and she knew his eyes were on them.

'Turn around, Cora. Don't be shy.'

She turned back to face him, one arm crossed over her bosom and one hand curved over her mound to hide the soft bulge of her bush inside the thin panties.

'Put your hands on your head,' he instructed. 'Don't you want me to see how close you shaved?'

'I don't have to play your games, Paul. I'm your teacher.'

'You won't be a teacher for long if I fail.'

Slowly, feeling the blood rushing to her cheeks, she raised the hand over her panties to her head, and saw his eyes glance at the shadow of her bush showing through the fine silk. His gaze lingered on the gentle swell of her mound stretching the delicate material before it travelled slowly up to her breasts again. 'Now the other hand,' he said.

She smiled sarcastically and stuck her tongue out at him, but she obeyed him and put her other hand on her head. Her breasts grew taut and she felt completely exposed as her nipples stiffened beneath his stare.

He reached out to touch her.

'Oh, no you don't!' She stepped back out of his reach. 'You'd better pass with flying colours, or I'll tell your mother!'

'We still haven't settled what the opposite of you punishing me is,' he reminded her quietly, and gathering up his sheet music, he left.

She had to take a hot bath, during which she teased her clitoris into three very hot orgasms, before she felt more like herself again.

The morning of the exam, Cora sat around her flat drumming her fingers. She had tried not to think about him since that last lesson, but she couldn't help herself. She hadn't exactly minded showing him her breasts and her pussy, not really. To be honest, she was thinking about that afternoon a lot, and thinking about it still got her excited. He *was* eighteen after all, and his eyes were so intensely grey...

The doorbell rang.

She walked to the intercom expecting the postman, and froze when she heard Paul's voice saying, 'It's me.'

'What are you doing here?' she nearly shouted. 'You should be in school for the exam!'

'Let me up. I've got something for you.'

Unable to think straight, because she was so surprised, she told herself, she pressed the buzzer and let him in.

Paul stood in her doorway speaking words she couldn't quite understand. 'Can't do it,' he said, 'got a job lined up in a guitar place. It's boring playing piano. I can't be arsed, frankly.'

'What have you got for me?' she asked softly.

'It's funny you should ask that, Cora. I've brought you a music stand.'

'But you're giving up music,' she said stupidly.

'It's got other uses, Cora. I thought you'd want to pay up the other part of our agreement.'

'Paul, please, be serious.'

'I am being serious, this is all very serious. The piano exam is just for you, not for me. None of it's for me.'

'I care about you, Paul.'

'You care about the piano.' He looked her over. She was wearing the same short, tight dress he had last seen her in, and once again she had decided against a bra.

'What do you want?' she asked faintly. She could feel it all falling apart around her as she stared at the music stand gleaming in his hand. What on earth had he brought it for?

'I want some reason to go on,' he said.

'I'm not sleeping with you,' she stated bluntly.

'Why not?'

'You're my student,' she replied weakly.

'I've left school. This is the last exam, and I'm not taking it.'

'You're too young.'

'I've been eighteen for six months now.' He shook his head. 'No excuse works, does it, Miss Brown? Don't you want to know why I brought you this present?'

'Come in,' she said.

The exam was at twelve. She let him in the house at ten o'clock, and to her vague amazement, she was naked by ten-thirty. She kept saying it was wrong, but her own body was against her. Even as her mouth made quiet arguments her hips shifted on the sofa towards him, her legs lolled open for him, and her tummy was exquisitely alive with increasingly excited butterflies again. She wanted to be naked. She wanted to be bare and open and exposed in front of this young man. She wanted to offer herself to him. She rose from the couch, and he unfolded the music stand before her.

'What's that for?' she asked dreamily.

'You'll see,' he replied.

She shrugged, and reached under her skirt.

He watched her slip her panties down her slim hips, and asked her to push her bum out towards him as she brought them down around her thighs. She did as he asked shyly, turning her back on him so he could touch her naked bottom. The breeze blowing in through the open windows cooled her skin even as his hand made her whole body feel warm. The cheeks of her buttocks felt as though they too were blushing as he caressed them. 'Go take the exam,' she said, 'and when you've finished, I'll...'

'You'll what, Cora?'

'I'll trust you,' she whispered.

'You'll trust me to take the exam?' he asked. 'Or you don't care at all about me and this is just whoring?'

She turned and undid the top button on his black jeans, and then the next, and the next. A moment later, she was completely naked and his jeans had fallen to the floor with a clink of loose change. The skin of his thighs was soft and warm against hers as he held her close, and ran his hands down her back to cup her bare bottom. 'What do you want me to do?' she asked softly, kissing his neck as he slipped his fingers into the knot of hair at the nape of her neck, and freed it.

'Bend over and hold the music stand,' he whispered in her ear.

'What?' She pulled away from him.

'This is the opposite of you punishing me,' he explained.

'What are you going to do to me?'

He reached down, and picked up one of his discarded trainers.

'Best get it over with quickly, Cora. You'll like what I've got for you after you take your medicine, I promise.'

Her face red with shame, Cora found herself bending over the music stand. The metal was cold, and she felt the cool spokes of the music rest pressing against her nipples. The breeze wafting in through the windows played over her pert buttocks, which felt exquisitely exposed as Paul lined himself up behind her, and swished the running shoe through the air near her hips. 'You won't hurt me will you?' she pleaded.

'Only enough to make you take it seriously,' he replied. 'Isn't that what you told me? You've got to

suffer for your art?'

'I meant practice...'

'Well, I'm going to practice on you.' He thrust his free hand between her thighs, and she felt his astonishingly skilled fingers reaching for her clit and playing with it very much as she herself had after his last lesson. He teased her and she felt herself getting wetter and hotter and bucking her pussy back towards his hand despite herself. 'That's it, Miss Brown. I knew you'd like it if you let yourself go.' He took his hand away, and brought the trainer down hard across her left cheek with a loud smack.

It burned like fire. She couldn't believe what a sting the rubber sole packed. 'Oh!' she cried in distress. 'You can't do that again!'

'Then I couldn't possibly take the exam. You don't really care, do you? If you can't take a little pain for your art, why should I?'

Cursing him through her clenched teeth, she bent over again to take her punishment. The trainer hissed through the air as she caught her breath, then seared her flesh again with another loud smack. 'Oh!' she howled. 'Oh!'

'Be quiet,' Paul muttered. 'Or I'll have to tell people you're neglecting your students.'

To her shame, Paul stuffed her panties in her mouth when she kept protesting, and then pointed at the music stand until she braced herself on it again, and bent over for more punishment. He subjected her to six more blows from the excruciatingly hard rubber sole, three to each one of her flaming cheeks. Then she was rubbing her sore bottom and blinking furious tears out of her eyes as she asked him to leave.

'Not yet,' he said. 'We've got time before the exam.'

'I want you to go!'

'Kneel under the piano,' he commanded.

For some reason, she obeyed him without another word. Then he sat down on the bench and played the Grieg, softly and beautifully, while she followed his orders. 'Suck me,' he said, and she knelt between his legs and reached into his underwear. She couldn't believe the size of his cock, and after seeing it she didn't need any further instructions. She licked his pulsing helmet, and a drop of pre-cum added a pleasant salty tang to the flavour of his skin on her tongue. She licked him up and down, tonguing his balls, and then sucked him hungrily, taking him deep into her mouth. The piano piece got louder and louder as she caressed his helmet with her throat, her eager and experienced tongue and lips urging him to come in her mouth as he played the final chords of the Grieg so she could swallow every last drop of his sweet come at the same time.

Afterwards, he went away for an hour to take the exam. Then he came back and got into bed with her and she opened her legs as wide as she could for him, sighing with pleasure as his erection sank into her blonde bush. He licked and bit the nipples of her sweet breasts as his strong young rod diving swiftly and energetically into her pussy made her ride wave after wave of pleasure. Then he turned her over and examined the still rosy cheeks of her bottom, making her blush all over as he slid a curious finger between them into her dimpled little hole. She came again helplessly as he finger-fucked her anus. After that, he made her sit naked at the piano and play the whole of the Grieg for him while he knelt between her legs and kissed and licked her pussy until she lost sight of the notes as she climaxed again. Nearly blind with pleasure, she kept playing the piano for as long as he skilfully kept playing her trembling, vibrating body, the notes ringing in her head and coming beautifully alive in her blood as she came again, and again.

Supermarket Slut

I like to tease checkout clerks. I've got thirty-six DD breasts and honey-blonde hair, and I like to wear low-cut sweaters at least one size too small for me over tight skirts - *really* tight skirts. When I go to the supermarket I always reach into my trolley, deep into my trolley, so almost my whole bum is exposed when I bend over, and the male clerks all look at me helplessly from behind their tills and credit card stands. And then I like to hold an item just in front of my big breasts. More often than not, my nipples are erect. I don't like to wear a bra and it's chilly in the supermarket, and I'm also excited by what I'm doing to all these guys. I stand there holding something, a little can of peas for example, in front of my chest, which the clerk I've chosen as my target tries hard not to look at as I bend down over his little plastic stand - to give him a good eyeful - and say, very throatily, 'These peas, are you sure they're marked the right price?'

He blushes, and very gingerly takes the can of peas from between my breasts. I always wear a short-sleeved jumper, even in winter, under an open coat. They call for the manager to come and check the price, or if the manager isn't around, they do it themselves. They get up, trying to hide the erection inside their supermarket uniform trousers, and step out from behind the till to go check the price.

It's always the same. I find cans in out-of-date displays, or a type of pizza that's just gone off sale, or a brand that's just like the brand on sale only a little different, and I usually get a refund. Only sometimes, and these are the times I like the best of all, there's no refund to give and it was my mistake all along and they apologise to me for the inconvenience. They mutter, 'Sorry miss, I'm afraid you'll find...' Or they say, trying to sound firm, 'No, that's the price, all right.' Or they might say, 'We can't find any other price label, madam, I'm sorry.' The point is, they all say they're sorry, and then look down at my generous bosom and smile slightly, glad to have me standing there while they hand me back whatever it was I had them pricing. I laugh happily in their faces, and then they all stare at my bottom in my short tight skirt as I walk out of the store. They all look hungrily at my shapely buttocks as I saunter out, all of them except for Ron, the manager. I rather suspect he's got it in for me, has Ron.

It started the day I saw the new sign behind the head cashier's desk on the way out of my local supermarket, where Ron works. The sign said, *Price Corrections and Verifications on Request. Client Privileges Applied.* I asked a blond checkout clerk whose nametag said *Damien*, what this new sign meant.

'No idea,' he replied, 'manager's special.' And he went to check the price of a can of butter beans I gave him. I was wearing shorts because it was summer, and hot. My long legs were tanned the colour of gingerbread; I had been away on holiday by the sea just the week before. Maybe Ron had cooked this scheme up while I was gone. I hummed, and Damien came back a few minutes later with the butter beans. 'No, that's the price, Miss Waterford,' he said, and smiled at my breasts.

'How do you know my name?' I asked, the first nervous peeling of alarm bells going off in my head. I can feel when something isn't right even if I can't consciously put my finger on it.

'My manager,' Damien smiled, still looking at my shirt stretched tight across my left breast where the strap of my handbag pulled on the cloth. Then he glanced down at my legs. 'He said that was your special price, Miss Waterford, and he has a Client Privilege reward to give you.' He pointed at the Service Desk overlooking the store.

I made my way, nose twitching with anticipation, to the booth where Ron sat in a white shirt with the sleeves rolled-up. 'Miss Waterford!' he exclaimed in apparent delight, smiling at me. 'How good of you to stop by.'

'You have something for me?' I said, tugging my handbag across my breasts. Ron was one man I didn't like teasing directly. He had a way of looking at me that didn't just undress me, it had me face down across a bed and spread-eagled with hand-cuffs at my wrists and ankles. That was the kind of look he gave me, and I didn't care for it.

'Client Privilege,' Ron stated, and slipped a gold card across the counter towards me. I reached out for it, but he plucked it back behind the glass partition out of my reach. 'Forms must be signed first,' he said.

'What's to sign?' I asked impatiently. 'Is it mine, or isn't it?'

'It's yours if you agree to the conditions,' he replied, and smiled at me over his glasses. I noticed that he had very large, strong white teeth. 'Would you like to agree to the store's conditions, Miss Waterford?'

'Yes,' I said, and promptly signed the form he gave me, because that's the kind of girl I am. I shop there every day. What could they do to me, bar me from the store? Not likely, not when they all live to see my tits. He handed me the gold card, and it was a store credit for a hundred pounds. I took the piece of plastic from him, and got all hot at the thought of what I could buy myself with it. I love chocolate, so I tottered off in my high-heels. I felt his eyes on the cheeks of my bottom, peeking out of my short-shorts, all the way across the concourse, until I walked past the tills and out of his line of sight.

I found out about the small print in the agreement I had signed the next day when I bought a giant panda full of chocolate. It was marked down, made of milk-chocolate and full of cream. I wanted it, so I took it to the checkout counter and paid with my gold voucher. Then I asked the clerk, it was Damien again, about the price. At that moment Ron appeared as if by magic from behind the adjoining till. He had a form in his hand. 'Miss Waterford,' he said.

'Ron,' I said.

'It pains me,' he began, shaking his head.

'Not half as much as it pains me,' I said. 'The bear's priced wrong.'

He put his hand under my arm - my bare, slender arm with its fine dusting of blonde hairs that all the checkout clerks had been drooling over for years. He not only touched my arm, he grabbed a hold of it and hustled me off into the cosmetics aisle, which was empty at the moment. Damien followed us.

'It pains me to remind you, Miss Waterford,' Ron began again, only I could tell it didn't pain him at all, really, 'about the agreement you signed...'

'Amanda, if you must,' I snapped, 'and don't touch my arm.'

'I am within my rights, Miss Waterford,' Ron assured me soberly. 'I can touch your arm, indeed, I can touch your head, your elbow, your knee, any part of your body I please. The agreement you signed, Miss Waterford, has been breached.' And he held up the form with my name on it so I could read the paragraph now circled in red: *Clients abusing the privileges of the supermarket-client relationship agree to compensate the supermarket with supermarket-client privileges at the management's discretion. Failure to cater to the supermarket privilege provision will result in prosecution. The client will compensate the supermarket for any costs incurred in levying privileges from the client.*

'What does it mean?' I asked, feeling a little sick and dizzy suddenly. Those small alarm bells were not just ringing in my head now, they were tolling ominously.

'You owe us privileges, my dear,' Ron replied smugly. 'You owe me, the management, Damien here, and a host of other checkout tellers up and down the aisles, as well as the shelf stackers and meat handlers and dairy inspectors. In short, you owe everyone. You've wasted the firm's time. That bear costs exactly what it says on the label, doesn't it?'

'Um, maybe...' I stammered.

'You knew that when you asked for the price check, didn't you?'

'I... you can't prove that!' I blurted.

Ron pulled small scraps of paper from his pocket, and I saw they were receipts, dozens of them. 'Thirtieth of June, thirty-first of June, the first of July, the second, the third, the fifth and the seventh of July, a break of two weeks - oh blessed peace - and then yesterday, and seven days before that... you have a record, Miss Waterford. You love to cost us time and money.'

'What can I do?' I whispered, my head spinning. I had signed the agreement, there was no doubt about that; my signature was swimming before my eyes. I don't like papers with my name on them, except checks made out to me, of course, and now I knew why.

He took me into the back room through wide plastic doors made of clear sheeting where the trolleys always come from, and Damien followed us in. We were facing a wall of sugar bags stacked on steel trays, hundreds of them. 'Count them,' Ron said.

'But there's so many,' I protested. 'I don't know where to start.'

'All right.' He smiled triumphantly. 'You want to know what you can do instead?'

I nodded.

'Make him happy.' He pointed at Damien.

I looked at the checkout clerk, and he looked at me... well, at my breasts. 'What am I going to do for him?' I asked quietly.

'Well, for starters, you could take your top off,' Damien replied, 'and climb on those sugar bags.'

'In your dreams!' I was in charge of myself enough not to let the tears burning behind my eyes make my voice quaver.

'Exactly, Amanda, exactly, in his dreams. Dreams are what we make come true here at the supermarket, in our small way. A chocolate bear. You were happy for us to give you that, weren't you, Miss Waterford? You were perfectly happy to let us *give* it to you for *free*. Having wasted all of our time as selfishly as you have for years, don't you think you should make at least one of Damien's dreams come true today? What will it cost you, a little pride?'

'I don't strip like a common tart,' I retorted, my face burning with an indignant blush. 'And I certainly have no intention of stripping in a supermarket warehouse. What do you think I am, anyway?'

'Is there anything wrong with supermarket warehouses, Amanda?' Ron glared at me over his glasses.

'Yeah,' Damien piped in, 'what's wrong with us?'

Ron then appraised me of the considerable cost of bringing a case to court. I don't earn that much, certainly not enough to even think of engaging a solicitor to defend me in court. He assured me that the corporate office would back him in his case against me. It hated all the man hours lost to sensation seekers like me. That's what he called me, a sensation seeker. Then he told me again to take my top off and climb onto the sugar bags. I blushed even more deeply, but I put my handbag down. Damien was standing right beside me. I protested again weakly, but Ron just looked up at the ceiling and sucked air through his teeth impatiently. I took a step back away from them both, and found myself touching the sugar bags with my bottom. I blinked tears out of my eyes as I gripped the hem of my top, pulled it slowly up over my head, and then quickly covered my naked breasts with it.

'I can't see her,' Damien said.

'Never mind,' Ron told him. 'Up on the bags, my dear girl.'

'How can I...? I mean, can I have a ladder, please? If not, I'll have to take my hands...'

'No ladder.' Ron smiled at me. 'We believe in getting on the floor with the customer.'

I turned my back on them, and was obliged to push my bottom virtually in their faces as I climbed the steel frame to the top of the sugar bags. A heel broke off one of my sandals in the process, but I got up there, and sat with my arms crossed over my breasts, dangling my bronzed legs down over the sacks. I could feel their eyes pulling my skirt up as I climbed, and now I sat with my pussy at eye level to them as they looked straight into my mini-skirt at my frilly black panties. 'What more do you boys want?' I asked sulkily.

'Take your panties off,' Damien responded at once, and smirked up at me.

'You'd be so lucky!' I snapped. I was flushed from the climb and still a little tearful, but I was also strangely flushed, not from the climb but with an excitement I could scarcely admit to myself.

Ron put his hand on my leg, cradling my calf. 'The supermarket,' he said, 'can reclaim property in lieu of costs, if such action is required. Aren't those the store brand? I recognise the gusset. I've receipts for every item of intimate apparel you've bought here for months, Amanda. I could tear your panties off you a thread at a time and charge you for my hour.'

I felt a tear of humiliation slip helplessly down my cheek.

'Take your hands off your breasts and show them to us, like a good customer,' Ron urged, his hand moving slowly up my leg to my thigh as Damien stepped up close beside him.

I bit my lip as I raised my arms and put my hands on my head. My breasts stiffened in the cool air of the backroom, and my nipples perked up even as I blushed with shame.

'Do you want us to charge you for taking your panties off?' Ron asked.

I shook my head, and was just starting to wriggle my hips to try and get them off without lifting my skirt too far when he thrust his hand impatiently between my thighs. He ripped open my panties as easily as wet tissue, slid them down my thighs, and tossed them behind him. All I had around my waist now was my mini-skirt, and both of them were staring avidly into it. I closed my eyes and tried to close my legs, but they wouldn't let me; they each grabbed hold of one of my ankles and made me spread them wide. Then Ron told me to get back down off of the sugar bags.

I turned around, and held on to the begs as I started climbing back down. A pair of hands - I think Damien's since they were so quick - caught hold of my hips and pushed my skirt up as I was coming down from my perch, so that now my bottom was as bare as a baby's. And before my feet touched the floor, he had found the clasp in my skirt and slipped it off me completely.

I don't know how long I was in the backroom that day. Damien's hands pressing on my shoulders told me I should go down on my knees, and so I did. I wouldn't open my eyes, I wouldn't look at them, but I knelt. And then somebody's cock nudged my lips. I don't know whose cock it was, but it was slick with pre-cum, like he'd been hard for a long time, and I parted my lips and it slipped between them, its engorged helmet pushing down on my tongue and grazing the roof of my mouth. Whoever he was, he moaned above me and held me down as I sucked him, controlling my movements by holding my head.

When I tried to finish him off too soon to get it over with, he pushed my face away for a moment, and then made me keep sucking him gently. I took him deep into my mouth, even caressing him with my throat, nodding my head like I agreed to everything he wanted, and when he finally came he forced me to swallow.

After that, Ron made me lie back across the milk trolley with my legs spread and began hungrily licking my pussy. I kept my eyes closed, but my clitoris eagerly sought his mouth, I couldn't help it, his tongue just felt too good. But then he pulled me up off the trolley, bent me over a cold stack of butter bricks that made my nipples painfully hard, and spanked me while he fucked my pussy from behind, smacking both my cheeks with each of his hands every time he thrust into me. I don't know who came after that, literally. I heard the plastic doors flap open as someone else entered the back room. Ron climaxed inside me with a great sigh, and let go of my hips. My bottom was so hot, I imagined it was letting off steam in the chilly backroom. Then some other man turned me around and suckled my breasts until I nearly had an orgasm. Then he made me kiss his cock, just kiss it once, and he came all over my face.

That was the first night. I still go there sometimes. If Ron is having trouble getting his clerks to work late shifts Saturday night, or to re-stock Sunday morning, he calls me. He says I'm the supermarket's Employee Reward Program all on my own, and that I should be honoured, because not every client has the same opportunity that I do to award privileges and make dreams come true as widely and as indiscriminately as the supermarket does. I know my place. I still get to tease checkout clerks, especially Saturday night, only the rule is, if he checks my price tag I have to step around behind his counter, get on my knees where no one else can see me, unzip his trousers, and take his cock in my mouth. And sometimes I have to offer Ron my bottom so he can bugger me, but he saves that for Employee of the Month day.

On the Rocks

My husband is headmaster of a school for boys located on a wild, rocky outskirt of land that juts out into the Nordic sea. It rains a lot and cold winds blow, so we don't venture outside very much, but my spouse keeps me wide awake at night. You see, he's a devotee of the cane. Even when boys aren't misbehaving, he likes to swish it about. He is very proud of his long white bamboo cane with the deep brown rings decorating its entire length. He swishes it this way and that, and it whistles through the air as he walks down the school corridors in his black professor's gown and mortar board. He can't actually punish the boys very much, because their parents pay to send them there and they would complain, so he keeps in trim with me.

At night we play this game. I slip into a frilly little teddy, and he comes to the bedroom wearing nothing but his black gown and mortar board. He is naked beneath his headmaster's attire, and the crisp hairs around his penis peep out between the black folds of his cape. He swings the white cane to the right, and I dodge it. He swings the white cane to the left, and I dodge it again. Eventually, he corners me at one end of the bed and I kneel down on it. He makes me pull the straps of my teddy off my shoulders and bare my lush breasts. My nipples are big as rosebuds, and he fondles me, running his hands through my hair while I kiss his cock. But it never gets hard; my husband has not had an erection for years.

The problems began when my husband's stepson, Stefan, came to stay with us. I had married his father the year before and never met Stefan until just before this particular holiday. His father purchased me from a mail-order bride catalogue for men who live in remote places, and for girls who do not have a much better choice when it comes to finding a good husband. I came from a family of four sisters and no money for a dowry. My new husband met me at the station where the little buggy that brought me from the last outpost dropped me. It was in the carriage on our way to the school that was to be my home that he first showed me his cane.

Stefan was blond whereas his father was grey, and that first night the three of us were together, we all sat down to dinner in the empty school. All the boys had been sent home that morning for a few weeks, and the halls echoed now with the ghosts of footsteps where we sat at one of the tables in the dining hall. Stefan was a slender young man with hot blue eyes, and every word he said echoed in the large, empty space.

He had an announcement to make. 'I want to devote myself to the cane,' he said. He was eighteen-years-old and would graduate from school that June. He was a man now, training to be a teacher like his father, and like him, he wanted to take up the use of the cane. 'I want to learn how to work a cane properly,' he went on very seriously, but strangely enough, he was looking at me rather than at his father. My husband was studying the ceiling with considerable interest, and stroking his grey beard as he listened to his son, who was eyeing the low, lace-trimmed neckline of my form-fitting black dress. From there his gaze travelled up to my blonde hair, gathered into a tight bun at the nape of my neck, and to my warm cheeks. For some reason the way he looked at me with those eyes of his - like blue ice that burned it was so cold - made me blush. 'I want to find out what the cane can do,' he added, 'I want to hear it sing.'

'You will have the halls to knock about in,' his father replied. 'I will lend you one of my spares. The old black India bamboo one, perhaps. That will start you off nicely.'

'Thank you, father,' Stefan said politely. 'I would be honoured to handle anything you have used.'

The trouble started the following morning out on the rocks. When the boys are away, I go out in the mornings to walk by the sea and sun myself on the rocks, braving the chill in the air for the pleasure of feeling the sun's warmth caressing my face and hands. My husband, the headmaster, does not mind my doing this, and no one sees me since the boys are all gone. It is a totally private stretch of beach and shingle beneath a looming cliff. Some mornings I even roll my black dress up around my waist and wade hip-deep into the icy water. Usually I take my panties off first and walk down to the water with my pussy exposed to the frigid air beneath my heavy black wool skirt.

On this particular morning the water was so surprisingly warm, and the sun felt so lovely on my face and neck, that I lost track of time. When I finally turned towards the shore and waded back onto dry land, my skirt hiked up around my belly, and my blonde bush shining in the soft morning light just out of reach of the waves washing over my thighs, I saw him sitting between two crags on the cliff-face.

'Stefan!' I exclaimed, blushing furiously and quickly dropping my skirt. The hem got wet in surf, but I did not notice; I was too captivated by the expression on his face as he leapt agilely off his perch, and walked down the beach towards me. The look in his eyes told he had seen that most intimate space between my thighs. 'You should have told me you were going swimming this morning,' I said nervously.

'I do not go swimming, I take the air, mother dearest.' I have no idea why he called me mother as he was my husband's stepson from his first marriage. 'And you were not really swimming either, mother. What you were doing was more like parading naked on the beach.'

'Stefan!' I gasped.

'You were,' he insisted coldly.

'I was... I was hardly...'

'Did you not show your pretty little pussy to anyone who might happen to be around, to *me*, in fact?' His eighteen-year-old face was hard, and flushed with an excitement made even more obvious by the bulge visible inside his button-down trousers.

'I did *not* show myself to you, I was just... it was an accident!' My cheeks were burning with indignation now, and my pussy was also strangely warm, perhaps from being the subject of so much attention, and of the conversation, which was exposing it in a different sense simply by acknowledging its existence. Normally, a woman did not discuss her most private parts with a man, and I could scarcely believe I was being forced to do so now by my own stepson.

'We shall ask my father if this is his definition of an accident. A headmaster's wife cannot be seen to do anything wrong. She certainly cannot be seen showing off her body like a common tart.'

'I did not...'

'Then how will you explain the fact that I know you have blonde hair the colour of dark honey between your legs, mother?'

'I will say...'

'He will put you on the next train back to that pathetic little village you came from.'

'My family would not take me back,' I said desperately, pleading with him by talking to him as an adult and master of the house.

'Oh, how terrible. You should have thought of that before you showed your pussy off like a harlot. Fortunately, for you, I have decided that you can help me with my work. Be at my room at nine o'clock tonight.'

'But I...'

'My father will be reading my school essays this evening, and tomorrow evening, and the evening after that, if I know him. He does not believe anyone could teach me as properly as he could. He will not want you in his bed until after ten. Wear the dress you wore last night to dinner,' he instructed, and then turned on his heels and marched away up the beach.

I felt as though someone had punched me in the stomach, and I felt tears threatening behind my eyes, but the deep cleft between my thighs made me feel as though I was still standing in the sea it was so strangely wet.

I wore the low-cut dress Stefan had demanded, but with a neck scarf draped across my cleavage. Just as he had predicted, my husband was in his study reading his son's essays. Why I could not have worn a more modest dress to help him with his studies, I did not know.

I stood at his bedroom door at nine o'clock trembling like a schoolgirl outside the headmaster's study. I had never felt this way even about his father, who actually *was* a stern headmaster. But his father had a penis that would not stand to attention no matter how long I licked it, and as I had already seen, Stefan's cock stood to attention without even being touched.

A moment after I knocked on the door he opened it, and pulled me into his room by an arm.

'Mother, dear,' he said, as I stumbled into the room. 'What is this?' He pulled the scarf off my breasts. 'How modest,' he said, 'and how charming.'

I blushed, unable to meet his eyes. His room was laid out as neatly as a young officer's quarters; everything was in its proper place. Only the covers on the bed were turned back, as though he had been about to lie down. And then I saw the cane laying across the sheets.

'Mother, dear, you see my cane?'

'I see it, Stefan.'

'Why do you not go and feel it?'

I looked at him for a moment, then went over to the cane and picked it up. It was black, and extremely flexible. As I lifted it the tip dropped down like a man's limp organ, and even the gentle movement of my picking it up caused a slight whooshing sound as the thin bamboo displaced the air around it.

'Lovely, is it not?' he said.

'If you like that sort of thing,' I replied.

'Do you not like the cane, mother?'

'I do not much...'

'I am sure my father has given you a taste of it.'

I looked at him again. He could not possibly believe... 'Your father would never...' I began breathlessly. 'He and I...'

'You forget my real mother was married to him long before you were. We were very close, she and I, and she told me everything despite how young I was at the time. I was only ten when she died. Lower the cane.' He took it from me, and laid it across the bed again. Then he whispered in my ear, 'I know my father waves the cane at you but that it does not bite. I know he could not get his dick up with a rope tied to it. My real mother told me these things.'

I stared at him, suddenly unable to find my voice.

'Take the cane up again and cut it through the air. Cut it through the air, mother.'

I do not know why, but I obeyed him without asking why he was making me do this.

'Make a big noise,' he went on, 'a noise like you're punishing someone.'

Tentatively, I raised my arm, and swished the cane through the air.

'Ouch!' he said.

I looked at him in astonishment.

'Cut it again!' he whispered.

My eyes wide, I cut the air with the thin strip of bamboo again, and this time the hissing sound was a little more menacing.

'Oh!' he groaned at the top of his voice, and then murmured, 'Again!'

I swished the cane perhaps ten times as his cries got louder and louder, until what I had feared happened, and there was a knock at the door.

'Stefan?' his father's voice queried anxiously.

Stefan leapt to the door and opened it. All of a sudden his eyes seemed to be shining with tears. 'Father,' he moaned.

'What is it, son?'

'Nothing... nothing at all. I am sorry to have disturbed you.'

'Has anyone...? Is something wrong?' My husband stepped into the room and saw me holding the cane. 'Gudrun,' he said, 'what on earth have you been doing?'

My husband gave his son the white cane to punish me with, the long, flexible white cane he uses himself in the bedroom. He gave it to Stefan and told him to punish me properly, as severely as he saw fit, across my bare bottom. It was the least his beloved son deserved as compensation for his wife's indiscretion. I tried to explain what had happened, but he would not listen. Stefan had told him I was correcting him for telling me I should not walk on the beach barefoot. His father said that what I wore on my feet was my own affair, but that I was not allowed to beat a man for any reason whatsoever. And he gave Stefan the white cane and his blessing, and went back to his study. He said he could not bear to see justice executed even though it had to be done. He said Stefan could punish me any time he wanted to for the entire week he would be staying with us. He had his father's permission to punish me until his manhood was satisfied.

And this is how I came to be in the position I am now, crouched on my stepson's bed with my bare bottom thrust up into the air. I have my face buried in a pillow while he administers the last of tonight's strokes. He gives me ten strokes every night, ignoring my muffled sobs. He prefers his father's cane because, he says, he likes to use the master's toys.

By the time he is finished punishing me, my buttocks are on fire from the ten long fiery welts decorating my cheeks and the skin just below them, the painfully sensitive area where my bottom merges with my legs. And as I remain kneeling on all fours, sniffing back tears, he runs his hands up my thighs to my pussy until I feel my burning skin melting into his palm. Then he turns me around to face the end of the bed and stands before me. His crotch is level with my face, and the size of the bulge in his trousers looks fit to burst all his buttons open. As always, I look up into his eyes and gasp, 'No...'

'I will tell everyone what I saw down on the beach,' he warns. 'You will be back on that buggy on your way to your mother's house, and you will feel every bump in the road this time sitting on that hard seat with your sore bottom. And father will not give you a penny, not even enough to buy some cream for your striped buttocks.'

'If I do this, will you let me be?' I ask ritually.

'We shall see, mother dear. Undo me.'

I undo his buttons. They are hard and black and shiny, like small coins, and what they buy me is the beautiful cock that springs out at me. The shaft is white as alabaster but the engorged head is a deep, lovely violet. He holds my head, and draws my lips down towards it. I pull back a little, but then my lips part and I take his young rod deep into my mouth. He bucks his groin against my face, fucking my mouth hard and fast, but he pulls out before he comes. I look at him a little tearfully from the strain of trying to breath with his helmet stuffing my throat, and because part of me is disappointed that I cannot make him lose control with my lips and my tongue. 'Stand up,' he commands.

I get up off the bed, and my long skirt falls down to conceal my nakedness. I feel cold inside despite my hot buttocks, and I want to cry.

'Come around here,' he says.

I go to him where he is standing at the end of the bed. I want him to kiss me and hold me, but all he does is turn me around so I am facing the mattress. Then he reaches around me and pulls my dress down with such force that the cloth tears and my breasts spill out of my bodice. He pushes me forward so I am forced to brace myself on the mattress and pulls my skirt up again, flinging it across my back out of his way. He caresses my legs again, beginning at my calves and moving up to my thighs, and then he runs his cool hands over my throbbing cheeks. My pussy is deep and wet as the sea by now, a fact his fingers seem to delight in pointing out to me as he slips them inside me, and makes me so desperate for him I want to cry again. Then he shoves me down across the mattress and pulls my welt-covered cheeks apart.

'What are you doing?' I gasp. 'No... oh no, please!'

'Mother, dear,' he says, 'you do not wish to get pregnant, do you?'

'I would not mind, with you,' I reply softly.

'Well, perhaps next time...'

I feel his turgid helmet nudging against the small, reluctantly puckered entrance to my anus, forcing me open and slowly filling me up as I have never been filled before. He stuffs me with him, fucking me like a whore and driving me to my first orgasm since I came to live on these rocks. His encouraging whispers hiss like the tide in my air, and his sperm trickles down my thighs like the foam of a violently breaking wave as I climax again.

Stefan takes me out onto the rocks, and makes me parade naked in front of him. Then we both walk into the sea, where he thrusts his penis into my body with as much force as the waves breaking against me. And then I kneel under the water before him, taking his strong prick into my mouth and holding my breath as I struggle to make him come as quickly as possible. I always swallow some salt water along with his salty seed, but I do not mind, and the cold air above the waves never tastes so good as that first ecstatic breath I take after he dissolves in my mouth.

Back out on the rocks, he has me lie on my stomach with my legs spread so he can enjoy looking right up into my most intimate places. He says he wants to see where I feel him at his hardest. He wants to see where I feel him when he enters me and possesses me. And I moan as his fingers part my labia and it all begins again, this time with me lying on unyielding rocks on my back, and then on my belly, being gutted from all angles like a helplessly beached mermaid panting with love for him.

An Exhibition at the Pictures

My husband and I like to go to the local cinema. It's a ramshackle place but the uncomfortable old seats have recently been replaced with good grey plush ones. The last two rows, that is, where we always sit, and pay extra. You have to pay for the best, don't you? If you don't treat yourself to what you deserve, who will? The story I'm going to tell you happened when my boy, Rory, was eleven. He wanted a party for his friends and we decided to have one at the cinema. They were all crazy about movies; Rory and his closest friends headed for the film club every Saturday morning at ten-thirty, so it made as much sense to have his birthday party there as to get sticky fingers over every breakable antique in the house.

I went to call on the manager, an old chap named Michaels. His bald white head shone as bright as the full moon under the hall lights, and his belly sagged over his belt like a bag full of marshmallows. I wore my blue suit and pearls when I popped in on him on my way to one of my charities. It doesn't hurt to impress this sort of person when you're looking to get what you want.

Michaels was the soul of helpfulness, and was completely amenable to the idea of a birthday party being held in his theatre. He would cancel that Saturday's film club, he said, and make it a private viewing for Rory and his gang. I asked him if he minded losing the business, and he said we could just make it up to him some time. 'I'm sure you will, Mrs Pennyfeather, I'm sure you will. It'll be a pleasure to see your boy get what he wants on his birthday.'

I smiled at him, and left. It made me rather uncomfortable the way he seemed to be staring holes straight through the front of my suit, and then instead of looking at my expensive pearls, he was busy studying my mouth. I do not mind men looking at my mouth when they are paying full attention to the words coming out of it, but Mr Michaels seemed a bit distracted by thoughts of what he might like to put in it. I could almost see him picturing my lips opening wider and wider to accommodate whatever lay inside his creased trousers, but I tolerated it because he was giving me what I had come for. I told him I would see him two Saturdays hence, and left.

The Saturday of Rory's birthday party my husband was away, naturally. He had given his son a great set of cars on race tracks but he could not make his party. Rory shrugged off my consoling kisses, so I said, 'Hey, the presents aren't everything, are they? You've got your party at the movies, and they're showing your favourite!' He cheered up a little then, and even smiled as he got out of bed.

We arrived at the cinema and found a sign on the door: *Closed for a special preview. Sorry for any inconvenience.*

We hurried inside.

'Mrs Pennyfeather, didn't you get my message?' was the first thing Michaels said to me.

'I certainly did not,' I replied. 'What are you doing with my cinema? I've got thirty of my child's friends coming in half an hour. You're not going to break my Rory's heart and tell him we've let him down, are you?'

'Well no, Mrs Pennyfeather, perhaps not, but it all depends on how much you can help me. I'll scratch your back if you scratch mine, as they say.'

'What can you possibly mean?' I demanded as politely as possible. He was looking at my mouth again. I was wearing a sleeveless blouse and a light cotton skirt. He took me in from head to toe, and then went back to gazing at my mouth as though mesmerised. I had chosen a soft pink lipstick today that made my lips look wet, and my blonde curls were freshly primped for the party. Rory's friends all have mothers, and so I naturally wanted to look my best. The cake was arriving in a van any minute now, and the last thing I could entertain at the moment was some randy cinema manager.

'This way, please,' he said abruptly, and led me into a back room where he showed me a clown suit. 'This is our alternative,' he told me.

'Where is my cinema, Mr Michaels?' I repeated. 'I booked your premises. We had an agreement.'

'The cinema chain called and informed me they were showing a preview here today. That's what my message was. There's no party. But we have another option. If you want to take your children in there after the preview, you're welcome to do so. You just have to keep them entertained for half an hour or so until the preview ends.'

'Me? I have to keep them entertained?'

'I don't fit in this clown suit,' he explained. 'It was made for a girl who works here Saturdays when the club's open. She does magic tricks.'

'I do not do magic, Mr Michaels. I am a woman with a position in the community, I hold...'

'If you'd like all your children to go home, that's fine,' he interrupted me. 'Otherwise, put on this clown suit and entertain them for a half hour. Here are some balloons. You can twist them into long sausage dogs.' He winked at me. 'I don't mind.'

I looked at him in utter consternation. 'Just half an hour?'

'You're a trouper!' His thin lips broadened to a grin. 'I'll look out for your cake,' he promised, and left to watch Rory for me while I undressed in his office.

I took my shoes off, and then my skirt, and I slipped the clown suit over my white bra and knickers. I did the big orange buttons up, and realised the suit was cut extremely low for a clown's outfit. Then I slipped on the big black boots. Finally, I put on the nose and the make-up. There was also an orange wig. I put that on as well, tucking away all my stray blonde curls, and then looked at myself in the mirror. Apart from my jutting bosom, I really did look just like Bobo the clown.

The children arrived a few at a time, and I got Michaels to swear a solemn oath that he would keep the mothers out, as I had no intention of being seen like this. He kept his word. The last thing I needed was Rory's friends' mothers commenting in the playground about what a wonderful clown I had made. There were about thirty kids in total, and once they were all settled down, I came out and blew a honk on my little horn. They were delighted, and they all seemed to like my costume. I let them pull off my nose and let the elastic snap back, and one thing led to another and I found myself shaking a tambourine and singing *Nelly the Elephant Packed Her Trunk*. They loved it, and by the time Michaels came out to tell me to stop for a moment so he could have a word with me, I was actually getting into it.

'Bit of a problem,' he said.

'You want another five minutes?' I panted. 'No problem.'

'No, I need you to do ten minutes in *there*.' He thumbed in the direction of the auditorium.

'What's the matter?'

'Projector broke down.' He sighed. 'Happens from time to time. Thing is, this is a special audience for a test screening. They'll get impatient and leave before I've time to fix it if I can't keep them entertained somehow.'

'So let them leave,' I said, not seeing the problem.

'You don't understand. If they leave now I'll have to get them to come back later and start all over again. That means no screening for your party. You'll have to go home.'

'No way,' I said.

'Well, you've just got to keep them entertained for ten minutes. Shouldn't be hard, with your gifts.'

'What kind of audience is it?'

'Oh,' he shrugged, 'just men.'

I left him with the kids, and walked out onto the narrow stage in front of the screen. The six front rows were full of men; bored, restless men beginning to feel aggressive because they weren't getting what they had come for.

'Hello!' I called out cheerfully. 'Would you like me to sing you a song?'

'Tell us a joke,' one of them yelled back.

'I don't know any jokes,' I said, laughing, 'I'm a clown!'

'Then what else can you do?' The same man demanded. 'You're certainly not funny.'

'What kind of movie were you watching?' I asked, unable to think of anything else to do or say.

'Dirty Debbie Does Dallas,' a chorus of voices replied.

I blinked in disbelief. Bloody Michaels! I saw him peeking out at me from the back of the auditorium, smiling at me through the round window in the door. It was a blue movie test screening audience he had me in front of!

'Well, um, where had you got to in the film?' I asked quietly, trying to wrap my brain around the fact that over fifty horny men were all looking at me where I stood before them dressed in a clown suit.

'She was just about to take her clothes off!' someone shouted. 'She was just about to get the shaft!'

'I see...' I swallowed hard, trying to think fast.

'Strip!' One of the men in the front row shouted.

'I could do some juggling,' I suggested desperately, even though I had never juggled before in my life.

'Strip! Strip! Strip!' The chant went up.

I just stood there.

One of the men, I remember he was wearing a raincoat, stood up, and a few others followed his lead. Michaels held up his watch to the round window, and pointing at it frantically indicated he still needed ten minutes to fix the projector.

'I'll take my wig off!' I declared. 'Would you like that?'

'Let's see you then.' The man who had stood up to leave remained standing in the aisle, waiting.

It's a strange thing, but I found it very hard to take that wig off. It felt like such an intimate act in front of so many men. I pulled up on the rough orange mop, and when my own soft blonde curls tumbled down around my face, I almost felt as though I was showing them the golden curls between my legs. And for some reason, they all gasped when my hair cascaded down out of the wig and I shook it attractively across my shoulders.

'Now take the suit off,' the man in the aisle said.

'I'll take my shoes off.' I found myself bargaining with him breathlessly.

'Go on then.'

I bent over, very deliberately pulled the lace out of the holes around the tongue, and then lifted my foot out of the boot.

They went wild. 'The suit!' they cried as the man standing in the aisle resumed his seat. 'Take off the suit!'

I took the other boot off slowly, and then Michaels was in the window at the back again silently miming to me that he needed even more time. Then there was nothing for it but to undo the big orange buttons over my chest and let them see my breasts and my dark, hard nipples peeking out of the white lace of my bra. I could tell they loved watching the clown suit slip off my shoulders and down my silky-smooth arms, at which point I turned and showed them my elegant back. They were practically howling in delight as I reached behind me to unhook the clasp on my bra, and with my back still to them, I slipped it off and threw it at them. A man in the back row caught it as I turned to face them again, demurely holding the orange buttons over my breasts.

'Somebody throw me my wig,' I commanded, and someone did. I caught it, and then deliberately raised my arms to put it back on and exposed my breasts. My erect nipples were pink as candyfloss, and I jiggled my soft mounds from side to side as I pulled the wig back on, raising sighs and groans from my captive audience.

'Show us your arse!' a man in the back row shouted as, once again, Michaels's face appeared in the glass pleading for yet more time. So I turned my back on them again, and looking over my shoulder with a sly smile, I let the clown suit fall down around my bottom. Then, my smile deepening, I pushed my knickers down as well. I was naked as I stepped out of the clown suit except for white socks that reached up to my knees and a red nose and wig. I wriggled my bum at them, and bending forward, showed them all my most intimate parts.

'Turn around!' they cried.

I obeyed, letting them all get a good look at my pussy, drops of moisture glistening in its blonde curls, and then I picked up my clown suit and hurried out of the auditorium, blushing furiously as I ran away from the terrifyingly exciting thought of being shoved down onto my hands and knees right there on the stage and forced to take all comers at both ends.

Michaels was standing in the corridor as I emerged covering myself with the clown suit. It was worse, somehow, being seen by this one man than by fifty. That had been a professional performance, this was too close to home.

'Don't put it away,' he said.

'I will, thank you!' I snapped, and headed for his office.

'Your clothes are in the projection room,' he called after me. 'I got the film going while you were out there.'

'Is it going now?'

'It is.'

I went into the projection room, and quickly put my clothes back on. Through the little window I could see the men I had just entertained enjoying Debbie getting shafted by a well-endowed man wearing a Stetson hat. A few minutes later, the picture ended and the men began filing out of the theatre. I ran a brush through my hair, and felt a little sad as I watched the children start pouring into the theatre with their mothers.

Michaels came in just as I was getting ready to join my son and his friends in the auditorium.

'Never mind all that,' he said. 'You can talk to them after their movie and give them their cake. But you must help me first.'

'I've helped you enough for one day,' I said. I was still feeling oddly sad as I glanced back at the clown suit I had draped over a chair in a corner. I almost felt as though I had left a part of myself behind in it.

He returned my smile. 'I can't get the projector to work for the children's movie, you know, not without the proper inspiration. It's a temperamental instrument, this thing.'

'You mean...'

'That's right. It only got going while you were naked. I don't know if it'll work without that kind of help again.'

'I don't know what you mean,' I whispered.

'If you don't slip out of that skirt,' he said, 'I'm not sure the film will run, and then no one gets their cake.'

We compromised. I put the wig on, and the nose and the suit, but not the boots. He didn't mind me staying in my white socks. But he insisted, if I was going to wear the clown suit, that he had to get out of his trousers. And while the projector whirred and projected a film about dolphins and their young human friends, I took Mr Michaels's cock between my softly painted lips.

He remained standing, holding the projector mounting, while I knelt before him in the clown suit and played with his balls. And in the end I swallowed and swallowed as he bucked and thrust and came in my mouth. Then he insisted I take my clown suit off after all, and I did. I dropped the suit along with my knickers, and bent over a chair. He patted my bottom, and then began spanking me slowly but firmly. I was surprised, but he said I should pay extra for the private screening from such highly qualified staff.

He gave me an extra hard smack on my left buttock, and then grasped me firmly by the hips with both hands before sinking into my pussy from behind. I gasped with surprise that his prick had gotten stiff again so fast, and then with pleasure as he stabbed me hard and fast.

'You know, you're a stuck up little madam,' he said. 'It'll do you good to carry the memory of this day's work on your bum for a while to remind you.' And he spanked each one of my cheeks again as he penetrated me. He stroked the soft hairs at the nape of my neck, and whispered in my ear that the fathers of the children in the auditorium now were the men who had attended the screening. He told me they would call me after I dropped my boy off at school and ask me to entertain their friends as well. I climaxed as he pounded into me while cruelly kneading my breasts, and I promised myself I would take the clown suit away with me when I left.

Mother-in-Law, Raw

I first started taking pictures of my mother-in-law in the autumn, when the leaves were all sorts of pretty colours. She lives in a house by the woods just at the edge of town, which means anyone who wants to can practically walk right up to the house without being seen. I call her my mother-in-law, but in reality she is just my girlfriend's mother. I guess if she had been willing to acknowledge that, I would not have gone after her the way I did.

My girlfriend's name is Pearl. She and I have been living together for over three years now, and her mother, Annette, my so-called mother-in-law, simply refuses to acknowledge that fact. When she writes to Pearl she never even mentions me. Last year, Annette and her husband sent Pearl a Christmas card that read, *May you have a lovely season, come and see us soon*. They did not invite me, Donnie, Pearl's live-in boyfriend. I might as well just be her dog, or her personal vibrator.

That's why I began wandering down into the woods near my mother-in-law's house. Her husband leaves for work very early every morning and she stays home alone all day. Annette is a very nice looking woman. Her bottom isn't too big, although it's been nicely lived in. Yes, she has buttocks you wouldn't mind getting a hold of, and she has nice firm breasts. I know that now; I saw them for the first time that autumn.

When her husband leaves for work, Annette has her coffee out on the patio, then she goes upstairs and takes a shower. You can't see her through the pebbled glass on the bathroom window, but I know she is showering because they don't have a bathtub. And I know this because they did invite Pearl and me over for dinner once, over three years ago, and they were even gracious enough to let me use their bathroom.

When she's finished with her shower, she steps back into view as she walks out into the corridor. That's where I got her with a telephoto lens as she crossed the stripped pine floor on her way from the bathroom to the bedroom. A window in the stairway lets in the light and looks out onto the woods, and it also gives anyone standing amidst the trees a clear view into the house. I got her once with a towel on her head and clutching a bathrobe closed around her. Another time, I got her towel-drying her hair and showing her face as she glanced out the window. A third time I hit the jackpot. I think the bathrobe must have been in the wash, because she stepped out of the bathroom with just a towel wrapped around her head and another one around her body. It was a big grey towel with yellow trim. She was massaging the towel into her hair with one hand and gripping the second towel closed just over her breasts. Then she must have slipped on something, because she let go of both towels to try and keep her balance as she skidded forward across the slippery polished boards. The towel around her body fell away, and I saw her perfect milk-white breasts with their perky pink nipples, and the golden peach-like fuzz just below her soft little belly. And while she bent over to pick the towels up, she slipped again. I snapped a whole series of pictures of her on her hands and knees on the floor naked, her mouth gaping open in surprise as though getting ready to take an erect cock.

I began sending her the pictures, one at a time. They came out lovely, especially the ones of her on all fours with her breasts pointing down at the floor and her bottom thrust up into the air. I mentioned in the typewritten note I enclosed with the photographs that her husband might, quite justifiably, believe she had posed for those shots. You can do wonderful things with a telephoto lens and a computer graphics card. Windowsills, even background walls, can easily be made to disappear. The photos I sent her could have appeared in a top shelf glamour magazine and earned her a few thousand pounds.

She replied to the anonymous mail box number I had given her. She sent me a note after she had seen just three pictures, the ones of her in her bathrobe. She wrote, *What do you want? I'll call the police if you don't stop.* That was before she got the ones showing her on her hands and knees with her mouth hanging open invitingly, and my accompanying remarks regarding her husband. After that, she sent another note that said simply, *What do you want?*

It is a wonderful thing to have an attractive woman with a jealous husband right where you want her. I wrote back to her that she should come out to the woods at midnight on the night of the full moon after her husband had gone to bed. As expected, she wrote back that she couldn't possibly do that, because he would wake up. She told me he was a really light sleeper. I sent her another photo of herself on all fours with her mouth looking like it was just begging for a cock to fill it, along with a sleeping tablet to give to her husband.

She left the house and entered the woods just after midnight. Through my infrared telephoto lens, I watched her walk out of the bedroom, and glance over her shoulder to make sure her husband was fast asleep as she gently closed the door behind her. Then I watched her trying to decide what to wear over the long nightgown she had on when she emerged from the bedroom. I saw her put a sweater on, and then she bent over the dresser on the landing to search the drawers. She held up a pair of sheer stockings, but then an owl screeched outside, and maybe she felt me watching her, because she closed the drawer abruptly and disappeared from my sight as she walked down the stairs.

She walked out into the woods and stood where I had instructed her to - a small clearing surrounded by bushes. You can see into the clearing from anywhere between the trees, but if you stand inside it, it is nothing but impenetrable thickets wherever you look. She stood there, just as I had told her to, waiting for instructions. I put down the camera and looked at her with my own eyes, practically holding my breath so she wouldn't hear me, and because she was so lovely. Her long blonde hair was hanging free, and even in the moonlight I could see that her cheeks were flushed. The ghostly outlines of her long legs were visible through her thin white nightgown, and she stood with her arms crossed over her chest looking as nervous as a girl lost in the dark. From what I could tell, she wasn't wearing any panties. This woman was just under forty-years-old, yet she obviously still possessed the romantic soul of a teenager, because even though she was old enough to know better, she had willingly left her warm, comfortable home and faithful husband to come stand out in the dark and the cold awaiting the commands of a total stranger.

'Are you there?' she asked softly, tentatively.

I said nothing.

'Are you there?' she repeated, and cleared her throat anxiously.

That same owl screeched again, and she drew in a sharp breath looking as though she might bolt.

I threw a small rock wrapped inside a note towards her.

She started when it landed at her feet, and then bent over to pick it up, giving me a nice view of her lovely bottom through her fine nightgown where I crouched just behind her and slightly to her right.

It was a full moon; she had no trouble reading the note. She did so, and then stood there for a long moment before she starting taking off her nightclothes.

The note had simply said, *Strip*. One word. I wasn't sure she would do it, but she did. I suppose she felt she had nothing to lose since I had already seen it all. But seeing a woman's naked body through a telephoto lens is one thing, seeing her taking her clothes off for you by moonlight in the middle of the woods is something else entirely.

She pulled her sweater off first, or at least she started to, but it caught in the clip keeping her hair swept back over one ear. She seemed to be having trouble disengaging it, so I stepped out of my hiding place behind a tree and put my hand on her tummy from behind to steady her. She gasped, and then seemed to melt a little as I helped her pull her sweater off. She stood with her head bowed and her back to me, submissively silent.

'Don't turn around,' I whispered. 'If you turn around, all those photos will go to your husband tomorrow.'

'I'll do whatever you want,' she whispered back, 'just don't hurt me, please. Just...'

'What?'

'Just don't let my husband find out.'

'What don't you want him to find out about?'

She started to turn around, but immediately thought better of it. 'I'll do anything you ask me to,' she repeated softly.

'Raise your arms,' I said.

She sighed, and obeyed me. Then all the breath seemed to go out of her as I reached down and pulled her nightgown up over her head, leaving her naked in one smooth motion. I heard her give a quiet sob as I pulled the clip out of her hair so its soft curls fell forward over her ear. She leaned back towards me helplessly, and sighed again as her body made contact with mine. Slipping my arms beneath her, I reached around and felt her breasts, pressing her stiff nipples against my palms. Pearl has large breasts, I don't know who she gets them from, but her nipples never really get hard. Now her mother moaned as I fondled her firm bosom.

Then I surprised her by slipping my thumb between her lips. I was feeling her up, and then suddenly I ran one hand up her neck and across her cheek and said, 'Open your mouth,' and she did. She opened her mouth for me and I fed my thumb inside.

I think she may have recognised my voice by then; I wasn't trying to disguise it. She sucked on my thumb quite ardently, and then I put my hands on her shoulders and pushed her down and forward onto her hands and knees like I had already seen her. She was crouched naked on the ground just like an animal as I sat down on a rock and unzipped my trousers. Then I picked up my camera and made her pose for me. I got her with my cock disappearing between her lips. First I took a picture of her opening her mouth for it, then one of her kissing it, and then another one of her nearly gagging on it as I leaned forward and thrust it down into her throat. I got a shot of her cheek smeared with my pre-cum as I slapped her face with my hard dick, making her beg for it. Then I shoved it back into her mouth good and proper and made her suck me like she meant it. As I started coming, I grabbed her head and fucked her mouth like a pussy, and I didn't let her catch her breath until she swallowed again and again, until I was drained. Then she licked my balls like a cat cleaning me without my even having to tell her to.

After those pictures of her blowing me, there wasn't much she wouldn't do for me. I made her bend over a rock and rest her cheek against a soft bed of moss while I took off my belt, looped it around my hand, and gave her a hard lash across her bottom with it. She cried out, but I warned her that her husband would hear us and after that she kept her mouth shut, just hissing as the belt kissed her flesh and she couldn't help sucking her breath in from the pain. I gave her six strokes, making each one a little harder than the last one. After coming in her mouth my mind was clearer, not so clouded by the lust her stiff nipples and curving buttocks and flowing blonde hair had aroused in me. She had been ignoring me, her daughter's boyfriend, for three years. She deserved to feel some pain; it might help straighten her out. After the first lash, I made her thank me for each blow.

'Thank you!' she gasped.

'What did you call me?'

'I don't know your name, sir,' she answered carefully.

'Exactly,' I said. 'You can call me *sir*.'

'Yes, sir. Thank you for beating me with your belt, sir.'

'You're welcome. You've got five more coming.'

And she took them, one after the other. There's nothing like the excitement of a woman who's been well behaved for too long. She'll do anything to feel bad. She'll even take a cock wherever her unofficial son-in-law wants to put it. Pearl has never spread her bum for me; she says it's too rude, she says her mother didn't bring her up that way. Well, this is what her mother did that night, and what she does on the nights her daughter is out of town on business. My mother-in-law, Annette, gets down on all fours in the woods outside her house and clutches the grass and moans as I slip my cock between her cheeks and make her squeal softly, so her husband won't hear, as I ream her good and hard. I tease her by saying that when Pearl and I get married, I want her to come along on the honeymoon. Then I tell her that when we're all legit, and she's officially my mother-in-law, that my brother will want to fuck her too. I'm serious about this. I tell her, 'He likes a woman who doesn't mind taking it up the ass and in the mouth at the same time.'

Annette groans and says, 'I'll do whatever you want, just take pictures! I want you to keep sending me pictures!' And then I come in her bottom and she comes too, shuddering and nearly sobbing from the intensity of her climax as she begs me not to tell anyone about what we do together. I haven't told anyone except my brother. I wonder what Pearl would say if she knew what her mother and I did at night in the woods with only the moon to watch all these timeless black-and-white images of human lust.

Foreign Secretary

Gloria Pryde, a voluptuous girl with plump breasts and long legs, was kneeling in the back of a luxury car with blacked-out windows on its way back to Whitehall. Her short skirt was around her waist and her tights were pulled down around her ankles and her breasts, pink as grapefruits and just as big, were hanging out of her low-cut angora sweater. Her position was a business matter, government business, an affair of state, if you will.

Gloria was the personal assistant of the Secretary for Defence. It was his limousine she was riding in half naked, and his erection that was in her mouth as she crouched before the plush leather seat and sucked and sucked as the Secretary of Defence caressed her naked bottom. Upon his insistence, she never wore any panties beneath her skirts. As always, he came in her throat, and as she was wiping the corners of her mouth with her fingers, and then struggling back into her tights and pulling her top up over her breasts again, the telephone rang. It was the Secretary's phone, the mobile unit he always had with him, just as he generally had Gloria. She didn't go home in the evenings like a normal PA, not if she could help it. Unless, of course, he was forced to spend time with his wife, by far his most annoying duty. But the telephone never left his presence. He carried it on his hip at all times.

'Tony!' the Secretary exclaimed with well-practiced delight. 'How nice of you to call.' He didn't say anything else for a few minutes, just gradually turned red under his beard and all the way up to his receding hairline. He was a small, trim man with a greying beard, and she had fancied him the first time she saw him when she interviewed for the job of his parliamentary personal secretary. She'd had ideas of her own about the meaning of 'personal', and they had taken exactly three months to define and execute. The Secretary's wife lived up in Carlisle, which had helped her considerably in her efforts to get his cock out of his ministerial trousers. Cocks, Gloria had found, rarely resisted too much if the women they rightfully belonged to didn't suck them regularly.

His face ashen now, the Secretary put the phone down. 'Yes, of course,' was the last thing he had said. Now he stared out of the window into the distance.

'What is it, love?' she asked. She called him 'love' when they were alone. She had begun doing so soon after she started pulling his zipper down, and he seemed to like it. It wasn't clear if he thought she was talking to him or to his dick, but then he was vain, like all the politicians she had met; he probably thought she loved his cock as much as his mind. She didn't love either one. Love never even crossed *her* mind as she swallowed and bent over his rod. She was a girl with a future to make for herself, he could help her with her goal, and that was enough.

'I have to leave her,' he said.

A pure, adrenaline thrill sliced through her belly and made her pussy go ambitiously hot. At that moment, she felt ready to fuck a whole troupe of ministry officials. 'Leave her?' she asked lightly.

'Margaret,' the Secretary said in a distant, distracted voice. 'I have to leave Margaret in twenty minutes flat, and then call them back.' He was still staring out of the window. 'Or I have to break it off with you,' he looked at her. 'Either way, they have to know, and they have to know now. That was Tony. A daily tabloid got the story. They're going to run with it tonight, and the party has got to get its response ready. So, I have got to make my mind up, fast. Good thing we had such a lovely holiday together.'

Good thing indeed, Gloria thought. His cock hadn't been out of her mouth for ten minutes, she had made certain of that. The man couldn't see beyond her devoted head bent over his lap, let alone think straight from all the endorphins swimming around in his skull from all those blowjobs.

He had come inside her on the beach, on the balcony overlooking the beach, even in the lift up to their hotel room. She had not let him put it in her bottom yet, but she had promised to let him, if he left Margaret, that is. If he left his wife, she would get on her hands and knees on the floor and lift her skirt like a good pony girl, and he could shaft her up the butt to his heart's content. She had not dreamed, however, that he might be collecting his prize so soon.

'Margaret is crucial, of course,' the Secretary was saying, his blue eyes still strangely distant. 'She's crucial,' he said again, 'to the progress of my career. The transaction of government business...'

'What am *I*, chopped liver?' Gloria snapped. 'What sort of business have you been transacting with *me* this past fortnight?' They were on their way back from Barbados, a fact-finding trip, so to speak, funded by the taxpayer and the British Council.

'Margaret undertook,' here his voice took on the usual air of gravity and fulsomeness it did when he was speaking into a microphone, 'certain imperatives that the usual ministerial aides cannot be called upon to handle.' He cleared his throat.

'And what have I been sucking?' Gloria asked sarcastically.

'Don't be vulgar.' He looked out of the window again. 'It's not like that.'

'I can do anything she can.'

'Are you sure?' he asked the scenery.

'Absolutely. I can do anything she can, and I can do it better, too. Haven't I been better for you, love?'

'It will be over between us the moment you fail me,' he warned mysteriously.

'Just try asking me to do something I can't do,' she said. 'If you can find something, then you can go back to her.'

'I can't go back to her. That's the point. If we make this official, you are the designated second in my ministerial work.'

'I can't wait,' she said breathlessly, flushed with success.

'All right,' he said, looking at her again, 'you asked for it. It's the street if you refuse to do anything I tell you to. We get divorced, and I'm finished with you.'

'What could I possibly refuse?' Gloria felt as though her entire body was grinning. She could taste victory like a bottle of sparkling wine poured directly over her naked skin.

'Let me speak to Tony,' he said into his mobile phone. 'It's the Secretary of Defence.'

She followed the Secretary, Derek, into his private flat in Bayswater. She had the run of his ministerial digs, and of course his private member's accommodations. She had handled his dry-cleaning, his laundry, his late night hand-jobs, etc. etc., but she had never seen his private flat. It was a basement one-bedroom off a side-street at the bottom of a flight of leaf-strewn steps, with a thick, dark curtain drawn over the one iron-barred window.

He switched on the overhead light, and she was overwhelmed by the smell of perfume. It was as if gallons of it had been spilled across the carpet. It was a small but plush pad very much like his ministerial residence, only here the bedroom was almost puritanically plain. The sheets on the wide double mattress were white, and only one pillow was propped up against the black iron bedstead. Hooks dangled from the four bedposts, and the only other furniture in the room was a tall dark wardrobe.

'What are those hooks for?' she asked.

'No time for that now,' he replied. 'We've got a briefing with the Chinese ambassador in twenty minutes and you have to prepare.'

'Prepare for what?' She was wearing a mini-skirt and a tight sweater with no bra. She couldn't imagine what a Chinese diplomat would want that she couldn't flaunt before him in this attire while fetching Derek's documents. That's all briefings were, rustling folders and clinking glasses.

'We're having that dinner with him later this evening to announce the arms sale. We don't have time for this,' he snapped. 'Get out the drinks.'

Gloria left the bedroom and found the drinks cabinet in the sweet-smelling living room. She opened the small built-in fridge, and snapped some ice cubes out of their trays into a small bowl before reaching for the bottle of vodka. Maybe Derek would calm down a little after he had a drink. Surely this briefing was nothing special, just the usual exchange of boring information and intoxicating fluids.

There was a knock at the door.

Gloria looked up.

'I'll get it!' Derek hissed. 'You get into the bedroom. And remember,' he added, 'I haven't divorced Margaret yet. There's still time for a reconciliation if you don't perform.'

'Perform what? I'll flash my boobs as I pass the glasses, like I always do. What more do you want me to do?'

'Just wait in the bedroom and open the wardrobe.'

Gloria went back into the bedroom, and opened the black wardrobe while out in the living room she heard the front door being opened, followed by a hushed exchange during which she imagined the two men bowing to each other in the Oriental fashion. But something seemed strange... she did not hear a third voice. No interpreter had been brought to the briefing. What matter could they possibly be discussing that was so clear to both of them that there was no need for an interpreter?

She was not sure what she expected to find when she opened the cupboard, perhaps some fetish clothing, perhaps some lacy lingerie Derek wanted to see her in after the diplomat left and he felt like celebrating. He always celebrated a bit of business by looking at her bare bottom. He loved to admire it and pat it and kiss it, although she had not let him enter it, not yet, not before she signed on the dotted line.

What she found inside the narrow black cupboard were scarves; black scarves, yellow scarves, red scarves; the wardrobe was full of multi-coloured scarves hanging from hooks. There was also a small pair of slippers lying in the corner that appeared to be made of black leather. She turned when she suddenly heard the two men step into the room behind her.

'Ambassador, may I present my *wife*, Gloria Pryde.' He held out his hand as if showing him a particularly fine car at a dealership.

The small, sleek-haired gentleman in a grey Mao suit bowed deeply in her direction.

Derek said in an undertone, 'Bow!'

Gloria blushed as she bent forward at the waist, flashing some cleavage at the ambassador in the process, but as she straightened up she saw that he wasn't interested in that. He was alternately staring behind her at the scarves in the cupboard and down at her hips. *Obviously, another arse man*, she thought.

Derek then began showing Ambassador Loo the wardrobe he was admiring. He ran his hand through the scarves hanging on the left side, and the visiting diplomat looked delighted. He also reached out to caress the scarves with both hands, feeling the silky cloth.

'Get us some drinks, Gloria,' Derek said through a fixed grin. 'I've said you're my wife, and you'll have to act like you are now.'

'Right.' She slipped out of the room, and tipped vodka into two tall glasses filled with ice. There was a lime in the fridge drawer. She cut a slice and slipped it in Derek's drink. He loved the tang of citrus in his vodka.

'Nothing for me,' Derek said when he stepped back out into the living room with the ambassador in tow and she turned towards them with their drinks. Ambassador Loo was holding four scarves in his two small hands, a yellow one and three black ones. They all appeared to be made of silk, and the black ones were embroidered with golden dragons. She had not noticed them in the cupboard and she wondered if they might have been in his pockets as he too shook his head at her offer of a drink.

'I thought so,' Derek said. 'Just as I expected. The drinks are for you, Gloria. Down one, *now*.'

'What?' He knew perfectly well she was not a drinker, not like his wife, whom she had heard liked the sauce.

'Get that drink down your throat, petal,' he said. 'It's expected of my wives that they drink. Anyway, Margaret always drank during the performance of her duties, and I'm sure she had a right to do so.'

'I can do anything *she* can,' Gloria retorted hotly.

'Prove it. Ambassador Loo is waiting to be briefed by my *wife*.'

'Fine!' Smiling stiffly, she tipped the glass with the green lime slice in it against her lips, and drained it straight off. The Vodka landed inside her like a wave of cold fire that felt very much like a punch in the stomach.

'And the other one.' The Minister smiled. 'My wife is known for being able to handle her liquor.'

Her head already spinning, Gloria Pryde drank the second vodka, and then, as if from very far away, she heard the dull thud of glasses hitting the carpet. The room was moving, and the last thing she saw was the floor coming up to meet her as she lost her balance and fell face down on the perfume-drenched shag.

Gloria awoke to a feeling of cold around her midriff. If she had not known better, she would have sworn her bottom was bare. She opened her eyes...

The black of the bedstead met her gaze. How odd. She could not remember the ambassador leaving, and surely she had not been out for more than a few minutes. Then she tried to push herself up, and discovered the scarves around her wrists, and the ones around her ankles.

She was trussed, a scarf at each wrist and each ankle, to the brass loops on the bedpost. Beneath her tummy there was a pillow, the one pillow she had noticed resting against the bedstead, so her face was pressed into the mattress. Now she could feel that the pillow was bent double under her, which had the effect of pushing her bottom up into the air. She also realised now why she had felt that sensation of cold about her middle when she awoke, because between her sweater and her high-heeled black shoes, she was completely naked. Someone had taken off her black mini-skirt before tying her face down on the bed. She was completely exposed below the waist, and when she looked over her shoulder, she saw Derek and the Chinese Ambassador standing at the foot of the bed behind her spread-eagled legs.

She blushed to the roots of her hair to suddenly see them looking straight down at her body's most intimate recesses. 'Derek, what's happening?' she asked anxiously. 'Cover me up.'

'Nothing is happening, my pet,' the Minister answered gravely, 'just the usual wifely rounds. And I can't cover you up before the deal is done. Don't you want to make a contribution to international trade?'

'I don't want him to see up my bottom!' she wailed. 'And why are you holding those slippers?' Each man was holding one of the black slippers she had seen lying in the cupboard. They were both gazing appreciatively at her bottom while bending the flexible leather soles. 'You're not...' she said weakly.

'We are,' the Minister replied suavely.

The Ambassador bowed, and swished his slipper through the air.

Gloria winced, and instinctively clenched her buttocks.

'Don't do that,' Derek said sharply. 'We'll want those relaxed. It hurts more if you clench them.'

'You can't do this to me,' she whimpered. 'I'm your *wife*!'

'That's what you *want* to be, my sweet. Well, this is what my wife Margaret has done for the British balance of trade these many years.'

'I'm not a slag!' she sobbed. 'I'm your lover!'

'Of course you are, Gloria.' Derek waved Ambassador Loo forward with a gesture that said 'after you'. 'But now you want to be my wife, and with such dreams come responsibilities. Relax your buttocks... there's a dear. And hold your bum up, it saves pain on your thighs, believe me.'

'Please be gentle,' she moaned, closing her eyes. She felt hands on her bottom, she didn't know whose, and added breathlessly, 'I'm feeling delicate,' as a finger traced the intimate line between her soft yet firm white cheeks.

'Not as delicate as you'll feel in a moment,' Derek assured her, and the first of the slipper's searing hot blows fell on her left buttock with a resounding smack.

'Oh!' she gasped, surprised by how much it stung.

'Not too bad, is it?' Derek asked. 'Ambassador Loo is clearly a man of refinement. He won't start you off cold. Sixty blows I believe is traditional in China.'

'Sixty?' She could not believe she had heard him right, and she looked up in time to catch an exchange of hand signals between the two diplomats. Derek was holding up his fingers and Ambassador Loo was holding some up in turn.

'Good news, Gloria,' Derek said, 'it's only going to be forty-five paddles with the slipper, but in exchange for the reduction, he wants to fuck your dear bottom.'

'No! Oh Derek, no! Please don't let him bugger me! Please!'

'All right, my petal, as you wish.' He nodded at the Ambassador and held up the finger of one hand plus five on the other. 'Sixty it is, and then we shall have to see.'

Gloria's bottom was glowing by the time the twentieth blow fell across her left cheek. Ambassador Loo considerately alternated between them, giving each one of her cheeks a moment's respite. Or, looked at another way, it gave the pain time to peak so she suffered the full effect of each blow. By the time the slipper fell for the fortieth time, across her left cheek again, she was weeping in agony, and with a terrible excitement.

'Care to renegotiate?' Derek asked.

'No! Yes... no more, please, no more!' She was panting with misery and lust. 'I'll do what you want, just don't give him my bum. But please, no more pain!'

'There has to be more,' Derek said calmly, 'but we'll see what we can do for you. After all, you are new at this wifely duty thing and you need practice.' On his signal, the slipper came down hard on her right cheek, and again on her left cheek, and then there was a blessed pause. She opened her eyes and looked over her shoulder.

The Chinese Ambassador was unzipping his fly, and she saw at once that he wasn't wearing any briefs. His stiff cock leaned out of his grey trousers at a rakish angle.

'Not my bum,' she squealed. 'Not my bum, Derek, please!' But the Ambassador was already intent on parting her cheeks. Then one of his agile hands reached between her glowing buttocks, and his finger caressed her most intimate slot on its way down to her pussy, readily accessible between her widespread thighs. She struggled against the scarves around her ankles, but she could not help it, his finger was exciting her. It astonished her how wet being spanked had gotten her, and her arousal was rising to a crescendo of desire as he dipped his digit in and out of her drenched slot. To her horror, she found her hips writhing up to meet his finger as it twirled casually around and around in her quim.

'Derek,' she gasped, 'how can you stand this? He's doing this to me, in the same room, in front of you! Oh, I'm going to come...'

But Derek wasn't listening. When she opened her eyes again she found his cock beside her mouth as he leaned back against the bedstead with his trousers around his ankles, and she knew he expected her to suck it. 'Where's Ambassador Loo?' she asked, because the exquisite teasing had ceased between her legs. She had been maddeningly close to an orgasm, but he stopped just before pushing her over the edge with just one finger. Then she realised where Ambassador Loo was as the finger that had been in her pussy pushed into the tight little rosebud between the cheeks of her bottom, lubricating it with her own warm juices and opening it up like a flower bud.

'No...' she moaned softly as the Chinese ambassador entered her slowly but inexorably, his helmet forcing open her virgin hole and filling her up. He seemed to keep sinking into her so she felt he entered not just her sex but her belly as well. And Derek took advantage of her gaping mouth as she cried out to press his cock down along her tongue, pulling her face towards him, and suddenly she found herself bucking helplessly between two officers of state as one came quickly in her tight-squeezing anus, and the other one shot his seed down her throat while she too climaxed despite herself.

The Chinese Ambassador gave her obliging bottom a pat as he slipped his cock out of her burning hole. And then Derek saw him out, zipping himself up on the way. He returned a moment later and untied her arms, and then her legs. 'Better have a bath,' he said. 'The Swedish Ambassador is coming to the same dinner. He'll be here in an hour with his two interpreters, who like to watch. Of course, then they want their own turn. Better spray some perfume on your bum. Margaret always found it covered up a multitude of sins.'

Border Wedding

Janilla was a tall, slender girl, and she was wearing white silk stockings that set off her coffee-dark skin and slim thighs. If you followed her long legs up and up, you would eventually encounter a skirt, a very short skirt as white as her stockings, and over the skirt you would be pleased to see a tight, low-cut short-sleeved white sweater whose soft, clinging fabric set off her magnificent 34D breasts, displaying the creamy chocolate fullness of her cleavage to delicious advantage. Her taut nipples just peeked through the thin material, for her sweater was semi-transparent in sunshine or under bright lights. Her large eyes were jet-black and usually as bright as polished wet pebbles, but today she was worried so they were slightly dimmed by anxiety. Her lips was beautifully full, although her mouth was almost too wide beneath her high Latin cheekbones, and today it was being nibbled on nervously by her startling white teeth. Her hands were tightly clutching her little white handbag against the front of her skirt as if it could protect her from the immigration officer before whose desk she was standing in the custom's office on the US and Canadian border. The officer wore a name tag that read *Superintendent*. He was an older man with a full head of white hair surrounding a hawk-like nose and a tight, unsmiling mouth.

'Why all the white?' he asked Janilla, not unkindly.

'I... I'm getting married today,' she replied softly, and then thought to add, 'sir.' Janilla thought it best to watch her manners because her passport was in his hands. It was an old passport from Paraguay, and the multitude of square immigration stamps made the pages of her visa section a red quilt of dates stamped by countless other immigration officers at a variety of exotic frontiers. Up until now, she had always made it through without being touched, even though she could tell the male officers were all just aching for an excuse to search her. Janilla knew she was just the kind of girl a border guard would love to have spread her cheeks so he could thrust a probing finger up into her bottom. Then, of course, she would have to spread her legs as well so they could thrust rubber-gloved fingers into her pussy, ostensibly to search her body's infinitely sensitive cavity for any illegal items she might be trying to smuggle across the border. That's what they called it, a 'cavity search'. What it meant was that someone had the license to put his hand into her most intimate recesses, to see her naked as she bent over an office chair and let him slip his fingers inside her, first into her rectum and then into her virginal vagina. So far, however, she had never been exposed like this; her pride as well as her precious hymen were intact.

'Getting married to whom?' the inspector continued his enquiry.

'To my sweetheart,' Janilla replied, unable to suppress a smile. Talking about her husband-to-be always brought a smile to her lips it made her so happy.

'Is he a citizen?' the inspector demanded quietly. His manner was still relaxed, but a slight note of tension had begun to creep into his voice.

'Yes, sir,' she said proudly.

'So, you're getting married for a green card,' he summed up breezily. 'I'm afraid we can't allow...'

'Oh no, sir!' Janilla exclaimed. 'I'm sorry for interrupting you, sir, but...'

'I should think you would be sorry, young lady. You should have a little more respect for the immigration service of the country you seem so keen on becoming a citizen of.'

'Oh, sir, I have lots of respect for you. I'm a very respectful young woman, sir, I always have been, it's just that I really do love my sweetheart. I'm not marrying him for a green card, not at all. I would never marry except for love.'

'Really?' The inspector's ash-grey eyes looked her up and down slowly. They took her in from the tips of her painted toes in their white sandals, to the shining black waterfall of her long, straight hair. She blushed beneath his scrutiny, which made the skin of her cheeks a little darker than normal. He was looking too closely at her sweater for comfort.

'Really, sir.' She swallowed hard. 'I love him more than I can ever express. He's everything to me.'

'Really?' the inspector repeated thoughtfully. 'Well, step aside out of the line, please. There are some irregularities in your passport I have to look into. Go into the office on your right, and wait for me.'

With a pounding heart and knees that suddenly felt a century old, Janilla walked down the sterile corridor and stepped into the office he had indicated. It was furnished with a small metal desk, two steel chairs, and there was a basin on one wall with a stainless steel counter next to it. Janilla felt her bowels clench uncontrollably when she saw the box of surgical gloves sitting on the counter, with one glove's smooth white latex fingers hanging half out of it. Stifling an impulse to run from the room, she forced herself to sit down on one of the chairs in front of the desk, tugging her white mini-skirt down as she did so to cover up as much of her long legs as possible.

After the longest hour she could ever remember, the inspector finally entered the office. She'd had too much time to imagine those lax latex fingers stiffening as they were pulled on over a living hand - by the white-haired inspector's hand, in fact. She'd had ample opportunity to imagine herself bent over that metal desk stark naked while he thrust his white plastic hand up inside her. She had pictured herself lying on her back on the desk, her legs spread wide open and her knees bent on either side of her face as she took first one, and then two, and finally a whole hand up into her completely exposed rectum, and then into her equally vulnerable and as yet unexplored pussy all on her wedding day. By the time the inspector arrived, she was willing to do anything she could to avoid a cavity search.

'I'm really sorry, sir!' she exclaimed as he seated himself behind the desk.

'Don't worry about it,' he replied mildly.

'No, I'm really, really sorry. I mean, really, *really* sorry. Just please... please don't search me, sir.'

'Search you?' he asked, looking straight into her eyes.

She blushed furiously, and glanced at one of the blank walls. The way he looked at her made her feel he very much wanted to slip on that rubber glove. 'I really don't want to accept a... a search, sir.'

'Oh, you mean these?' The inspector smiled as he reached over for the box of gloves, and set it on the desk between them.

'Yes,' her eyes were irresistibly drawn to the dreaded box, 'those...'

'Well, Janilla, if you don't want a cavity search to prove you're not trying to smuggle anything, and you can't persuade me you're not marrying for a green card, how do you propose to get into the country?'

'My sweetheart loves me,' she answered softly but fervently, 'and he'll testify for me. He'll tell you I'm genuine. He'll tell you how much he loves...'

'Men lie.' The inspector cut her short. 'All men are capable of lying for money,' he elaborated. 'Commonest thing in the world, green card weddings. People accept bribes, and the happy couple are two states away from each other before the ink's even dry on the marriage license. I've seen it happen too many times to believe in love any more. You'll have to come up with something better than that.'

'But...' Janilla was appalled. 'I love him! I love him with all my heart! I love him deeply. What more can I possibly say than that?'

'Can you prove it?'

'I love him like my own brother, like...'

'If you love him like a brother,' the inspector interrupted her again derisively, 'I definitely won't stamp your passport.'

'*Signor*, please, forgive me, it is just a Spanish expression, I didn't mean... I love my sweetheart with all my heart as a woman. When we are married, I will be a dutiful wife to him. I will give him all the pleasures a man could possibly hope to have in this world. I will love him wildly and passionately with all my heart and soul, *signor*.'

'Oh?' the inspector did not look impressed by her ardent little speech.

'Yes!' Janilla's nostrils flared and her eyes burned like coals. 'My sweetheart is a very lucky man. I will love him as only truly good and worthy men have the good fortune to be loved. He will be the happiest man alive come dawn tomorrow.'

'Show me,' the inspector said.

'What?' She had no idea what he could possibly mean by that request. Or she simply did not allow herself to understand.

'Show me how much you love your husband... your husband-to-be, that is. If you're going to show him a good time and be a good and dutiful wife to him, maybe you should practice a little first. We call it a rehearsal. But first you can have an audition, if you like, right here on the border, before you become another lucky American bride.'

Janilla's face burned as though he had slapped her on both cheeks. She could not believe what he was saying. 'You want me to...?' she could not bring herself to voice the completely unthinkable.

'Your sweetheart can come swear until he's blue in the face that he loves you, and you love him. As far as I'm concerned, money speaks louder then words. But if you can convince me you'd love him like a man deserves to be loved, I may not have to take out this rubber glove here and check you out for any illegal items you may be hiding between your sweet hot cheeks.'

Janilla could barely control the terror and indignation rising up from her heart into her throat and rendering her speechless. The room seemed to be spinning around her...

'However, if you prefer,' the inspector went on as he reached for the glove, 'we can go the traditional route.'

'No,' she gasped. Vaguely, she realised she was in shock.

'Very well then, the rehearsal for your wedding night can start right here, right now. Raise your arms so I can take off your top.' He got up from behind the desk and pulled the blinds closed over the window, which heightened Janilla's fear even though she was thankful her shame would not be exposed to anyone who happened to be passing by. If she was going to take off her clothes, she was grateful to be able to do so in private. As if in a dream, she raised her arms, and he pulled the sweater off over her head. Her breasts were full round chocolate mounds, and they quivered softly as they fell back against her chest after being abruptly released from the sweater's tight confines. The inspector's hands reached out to feel them, and somehow she checked her impulse to shrink away from his touch.

Her own hands gripped the sides of the chair and she turned her face away as his hands closed over her bosom. He massaged her nipples with his palms, and to her consternation, she couldn't stop them from becoming as hard as mocha beans beneath his firm, circular caresses. And she was even more horrified to feel a sweet warmth spreading across her vulva and taking smouldering root in her pussy. She had not been touched in a long time, and her body was responding hungrily to all this attention.

'Your stockings now,' the inspector said huskily, stepping back to watch her.

She put one of her sandals up on the empty chair beside hers, and pulled her short skirt up to expose her white lace garter belt.

'Mm, maybe he is a lucky man,' the inspector said quietly. 'We'll see.'

'I wore all these things just for him.' Janilla was on the verge of tears. 'He's outside, waiting for me.'

'Do you want him to see you doing this?'

'No,' she gasped. It would be the end of their relationship if her fiancé ever found out about this, if he ever learned that she had shown her body to another man. All this time, she had saved herself for him, it was one of the reasons he wanted to marry her. The marriage would be off in a second if he ever found out another man had beaten him to her treasure.

The inspector helpfully pulled off her sandals for her as she slipped off her stockings one at a time. 'Now, stand up, turn around, pull your skirt up and show me your bottom.'

'You won't...?' Her top was gone, her stockings were gone. All she had left to protect her was her skirt, a few inches of thin white cotton, and a delicate pair of white lace panties that were more for sensual decoration than anything. 'You won't... you won't make me feel the glove, will you?' she begged softly.

'That all depends on you,' the inspector replied, 'and on how persuasive you are. Lift your skirt up, push your panties down, and bend over the desk.'

Closing her eyes, Janilla did as he said. First she grasped the hem of her skirt with trembling hands, and then with a brave tug she yanked it up around her hips. He got an enticing glimpse of her dark bush veiled by white lace before she turned around to face the desk. Keeping her eyes closed, she thrust her bottom out a little towards his hungry gaze, and then she reached up and pushed her panties down over the smooth cheeks of her coffee-coloured bottom as he drank in the luscious sight before him. She slipped her panties down her shapely thighs to her knees.

'Leave them there,' he said firmly.

She was as embarrassed as if she had been caught going to the toilet. She felt one of his hard, dry hands cup her right cheek and weigh its soft, full curve. 'Please, no glove...' she whispered.

'Then I'll have to use something else,' the inspector said, and she heard the sound of a man's fly being unzipped. It was not a sound she was familiar with, but there was no mistaking it. 'You have to convince me just how much you'll love the man you marry,' he went on, almost gently. 'You can show me that, and I can find that out, without using a glove. Do you love your husband-to-be?'

'I love him very much, signor,' Janilla answered, and bent over the desk, her eyes still stubbornly closed so she wouldn't have to see what was happening, which might help her forget it later. If she could keep her eyes shut the whole time, there would be no images of her humiliation to torment her later, only feelings, and feelings she could suppress and forget, somehow.

Then she gasped as she felt something brush the cheeks of her buttocks and insinuate itself between them, reaching for her most private hole, and what she was feeling was definitely not a finger...

'How much will you love him?' the voice asked thickly.

'As much as any man can be loved, signor, I swear...'

'Then hold your cheeks open for me,' the inspector commanded. 'Show me how deeply you love.'

Janilla bit her lip, and obeyed him. She reached back and gripped her full dark cheeks with both hands, lifting her bottom up as she pulled them open for him, exposing the dimpled opening nestled between them. She knew he could see it when she felt cool air caressing it, a sensation it was not accustomed to, and which was not entirely unpleasant.

'No glove, my precious?' he whispered in her ear. 'You're quite sure?'

'No, signor, please, I beg of you,' she whispered.

'You leave me no choice then.'

She couldn't be sure, but she thought she heard a small break in his voice, and then suddenly she felt one of his fingers spreading something smooth and cold around her little hole. It stung somewhat, but then the finger was gone and she caught her breath as he moved in tightly behind her. He grasped her hands, and bending over her held them flat against the desk. She did not need them to separate the cheeks of her bottom any more because something else had been introduced to hold them apart. Her buttocks were speared open by the rigid penis pushing slowly into her anus. It thrust hard through her resistance, and then suddenly sank all the way into her stunned rectum. She sobbed with shock and confusion as it slipped all the way back out of her again. It was all she could do not to scream; his gradual withdrawal hurting her. It was a perverse relief when he sank swiftly into her body again, because for some reason it felt better than when he pulled out. When he was lodged deep inside her, she felt sickeningly stuffed by his dick but the burning torment was not as great. It took all her willpower to keep quiet as he began moving in and out of her, and judging by his groans, he was enjoying himself immensely at her expense. She moaned too, overwhelmed by all the sensations flooding her, not knowing what to make of them until one of his hands slipped down over the thick black curls of her bush and found her swollen clitoris. She was shocked to realise that she was wet down there.

Despite her pain and humiliation and her fear of what would happen to her plans for the future if her husband-to-be found out about this, she was so wet it was as if her pussy was weeping in shame of how aroused she was against her will. The inspector stroked her clit with his fingers, and biting her lip in order not to scream, Janilla felt as though some divine bomb exploded directly between her thighs as she climaxed. She came in long, helpless shudders as the inspector shot round after round of his milky seed into her hot chocolate bottom.

When she had tidied herself up, put her skirt, stockings and top back on, reapplied fresh make-up to her tear-streaked cheeks and thanked the inspector for being so kind and understanding, Janilla once more sat demurely before his stainless steel desk as he studied her passport again. She felt utterly drained, but soon, very soon, she would be out of this office and on her way to her wedding and her American citizenship.

'Of course, that only proved you're good in bed, not that you love him,' he said as he turned the pages of her passport, lying open before him on the cold metal desk. He had not yet reached for his date stamp.

'What do you mean?' she asked, even though she felt too strangely numb to really care; she could barely take in what he was saying.

'You could be a hooker,' the inspector explained, 'a professional. What you did for me isn't love at all. Or it might be. You came too, I believe? You enjoyed yourself, did you, my little wanton?' He smiled at her.

'What do you want from me?' Janilla whispered in despair. 'I love my husband. I'll love him until the day I die, if I ever get a chance to, that is. How else can I prove it to you?'

'What more would you do for him?' the inspector asked softly.

'Haven't I shown you already just what I'll do for him?' Janilla was close to sobbing with frustration and exhaustion. 'You were in... you were in my...' She broke off. It was too shameful to say out loud. She could still feel his hot breath on the back of her neck, and his fingers working between her legs.

'But you enjoyed that,' he insisted. 'Your own body showed you up. You came, my little slut. No, we need some more hard evidence, something to show you really care.'

'What?' Janilla asked faintly.

'Hold out your hand.'

Past thinking, totally bewildered, Janilla held out her hand.

'Put on this glove.' He pulled one of the latex gloves out of the box, and she slipped it on over her right hand. It was sticky despite the talc that had been pre-sprinkled inside the wrist, and hard to get one. 'Now, give yourself a little inspection,' he instructed, 'just for the record.' And then he took a camera out of the desk drawer, an instamatic with a large flash.

'I don't understand,' Janilla said stupidly.

'Drop your panties and put your finger up your ass.' The inspector was losing patience. 'We have procedures here, and you haven't been punished yet.'

'Punished for what?' she wailed. 'I did everything you told me to.'

'If you really love him, you'll take punishment for him,' he explained evenly, as patiently as if he was speaking to a child. 'It's not just fun and games, marriage. Sometimes there's pain involved.'

'I won't give myself a cavity search,' Janilla said hotly. 'I won't.' It was all just too much, and suddenly she was much more furious than frightened.

'Then you'll go back home to Paraguay,' the inspector retorted lightly, 'and your wedding night will have been with me. I'm the lucky man.'

Once again, Janilla dropped her panties, and once again she pulled open the cheeks of her buttocks, but this time she slipped a cool, gloved finger into her anus while the flash went off. The inspector took pictures of her beautiful face looking proudly defiant, and then deeply ashamed as she probed her own asshole. Then he put the camera down to spank her. 'It's traditional,' he told her. 'In our country, a bride usually gets a spanking from her father the night before she begins her life with another man,' he lied through his teeth.

'Is that true?' Janilla went wide-eyed with amazement.

'Oh yes,' he assured her. 'You'd better tell your new husband to punish you almost every day, or you won't be allowed to stay in this country.'

'Thank you, signor, I will remember that.'

'My pleasure,' he said. 'Now bend over and touch your toes.'

Janilla winced when his open hand made contact with her cheeks. He spanked her slowly and methodically until her buttocks were burning and the painful warmth was flooding her pussy in a frighteningly pleasurable way.

'You're almost ready to start married life,' the inspector told her. 'Almost.'

'What more do I need to do, signor?' Janilla asked as she pulled her panties up over her smouldering cheeks and smoothed her white skirt down over her thighs in an effort to restore her pure, virginal image.

'You must learn to use your mouth like an American bride,' the inspector informed her. 'Get on your knees.'

And Janilla knelt, taking great care not to run her white stockings as the inspector unzipped his pants a second time and her beautiful lips parted to accept his cock. She took it into her mouth and sucked hungrily on the taste of her life to come, swallowing mouthful after mouthful of her future as a married woman in 'the land of the free'.

All dressed in white, with another man's sperm seeping onto the insides of her thighs, she went past the immigration line to meet her husband - tugging her skirt down over the white lace panties sticking to her warm wet vulva, the cheeks of her bottom burning like hot coffee - a freshly spanked virgin tender to the touch everywhere.

Under the Lights

Anna Li was an extremely slender young woman, and she was a good five-feet-ten, which gave her thinness an almost ethereal air. She had a spiky mop of jet-black hair, barely long enough to put back in a ponytail, and she wore comfortable rice slippers everywhere, but she was tall enough not to need heels to set off her shapely legs, which seemed to go on forever. Her breasts were small, but her slim torso made her bosom seem bigger than it was below her wide, pouting lips. The extreme slightness of her arms emphasised the round fullness of the spheres beneath her shirt that bounced freely since she never wore a bra.

Anna Li's breasts were safely tucked away this morning for her audition, a particularly gruelling audition for a very important musical body, *The Young Violinists' Trust*. Her instrument banged gently against her thigh as she made her way up the long winding staircase of Wigmore Hall - all polished wooden panels and teak over plush red-and-gold carpets - to the small audition waiting room at the top of the stairs. She was wearing a very fetching short-sleeved silk blouse, a short navy blue skirt that fell to just above her knees, and today in place of her rice slippers she had slipped on shiny black patent-leather shoes over knee-high white socks. Friends had told her to go for the 'little girl look' which sometimes helped at auditions, and even though she did not understand why that should be the case, she took every advantage she could get, especially since it went along with her usual habit of not wearing a bra. Her light-brown nipples, hardened by the exertion as she hurried up the stairs, flashed darkly through her delicate white blouse, and becoming pleasantly aware of them, she hoped they too would stand her in good stead.

'Through there,' a severe woman at the top of the stairs said, and Anna stepped into the waiting room. Pictures hung on every wall of famous musicians, most of them dead already, and she wondered if anyone still alive could be considered good enough to play in these august surroundings. Then almost at once she got her call, and her belly churning, the neck of her violin a little slippery in her hand, she stepped through the great white door into a small corridor and from there onto the large, open stage beneath the lights. Beyond their bright halo lay the great black empty auditorium, and in it somewhere sat the person who would be auditioning her.

She blinked, unable to see beyond the great spotlights trained directly on her where she stood in the middle of the stage behind the music stand. She raised a hand up to her eyes and tried in vain to see out into the black auditorium.

'Miss Li.' A voice rose out of the seemingly vast darkness, a man's voice, deep and firm. 'It says here that you will be eighteen next month, only just making the qualification guidelines for this particular award. Are you sure you are in the right place?'

'Um, I think so,' Anna replied. She had not expected this question. She had expected simply to play, not to discuss her application with the judge.

'You are not dressed like an eighteen-year-old,' he observed.

'I...' Anna's mind reeled. She could not tell him what she had been told, or admit that she had worn a short skirt and a half transparent blouse in the hope of gaining an advantage with them. And yet she had to say something. 'I like to feel comfortable when I'm playing,' she muttered.

'Do you? Very well then, proceed. And mind you, be sure to play comfortably.'

Anna's bow felt strangely leaden in her hand; she could never remember it feeling so heavy. It was suddenly so heavy that it might have been a piece of timber just fallen off a builder's lorry she was expected to lift over delicate strings and make beautiful music with. And her violin, as she brought it up and tucked it between her shoulder and her chin, felt strange to her, as though it was alive, as though it was a hand touching her on the neck, a man's hand... Perhaps it was the invisible eyes staring out at her from the impenetrable darkness before her, and the act of obeying the commands of a disembodied voice that made her so intensely conscious of her own body. She swallowed hard, attempting to digest these strange sensations without letting them distract her, and tried to pull herself together.

'Is anything the matter, Miss Li?' the voice enquired patiently.

'No, sir,' she said quickly, 'I'm fine.'

'Are you sure?'

'Yes, absolutely sure, sir.'

'Well?'

'I'm sorry... I'm just nervous, I guess.'

'Everyone gets nervous,' the judge answered, still sounding patient, 'that is the point of auditions, to see how you react under pressure, to find out what you are made of. Are you sure you are comfortable enough to play?'

'Oh, yes.'

'Because if you are not,' the voice went on remorselessly, 'perhaps there is something I can do for you to make you feel more *comfortable*. Within reason, of course.'

'Thank you,' Anna said, confused by the offer, 'but I'm fine, really.'

'Well then play. *Now*,' the voice said more firmly, a sour note of impatience ringing in its melodious depths.

She had no choice, she had to begin playing.

It was awful. The first piece went relatively well, and the second wasn't going too badly, but then the distracting sound started. It sounded like papers rustling in the orchestra pit below the stage, or perhaps in the front row of seats, a crisp, persistent noise that disrupted her concentration, taking her focus away from the music as she wondered if the judge was bored and leafing listlessly through her application papers while he waited for her to finish so he could tell her she had not passed the audition. Her nerves snapped like brittle old strings, and after that it was terrible. The piece fell apart in her hands and the bow felt like a fallen branch she was scraping across an empty box. She felt tears burning in her eyes because she had failed, she knew it in her bones even as she continued to play. She would not get the award, and she would no longer be able to afford studying the violin.

'Miss Li,' the judge's voice rose out of the darkness as she finished one piece and, her teeth clenched, prepared to launch into another, 'I think you can stop right there.'

Anna Li heaved a silent sob. She couldn't help herself. His comment made it official - she had failed. He didn't even want to hear the rest of her programme she had played so badly.

'I think,' the voice said again, 'that you did well to wear what you felt comfortable in, only I think you did not go quite far enough.'

Anna was too busy feeling miserable to even begin to understand what he meant by that. She had failed. She would never play the violin again. And how would she face her mother, who was so proud of her talented daughter?

'Perhaps you would consider following my advice during the last piece in your program?'

She focused on what he was saying again. He wanted to hear her play the rest of her programme? She wasn't so bad after all? She hadn't failed completely yet?

'Perhaps I can help bring out the best in you,' the voice went on magnanimously, 'under these difficult circumstances.'

'I'll do anything you suggest, sir.' Anna blinked gratefully into the spotlights. 'Anything.'

'I am pleased to hear that. Take off your skirt.'

'I beg your pardon, sir?'

'You heard me,' the voice replied firmly. 'However, in case your hearing is remarkably poor for a musician, I will deign to repeat myself. Take off your skirt.'

'I...' Anna's mind was definitely reeling now. She could scarcely believe what he was telling her to do, and yet she was desperate not to blow what might be a real chance to save the audition, and her career as a violinist.

'You wanted to be *comfortable*,' the judge went on smoothly, sounding completely untroubled by her stunned discomfiture. 'If you want me to listen to the rest of your program, I suggest you follow my suggestions as to what will make you feel more comfortable. Take your skirt off. It looks quite tight, and I suspect it may be interfering with your circulation somewhat, whereas it is having the opposite effect on mine.'

Anna squinted into the darkness behind the blinding lights, decided she couldn't face her mother if she didn't get the scholarship, and unzipped the side of her blue skirt. It slipped down easily over her slim hips, and she stepped out of it trying to imagine that she was alone in her room and not on a stage. Then she stood with her violin held strategically in front of her cotton bikini panties, white panties to match her socks. A breeze seemed to waft across the stage from the dark wings, and her legs trembled slightly as it caressed her bare skin.

'Are you a bit more comfortable now?' the voice enquired.

'Yes, thank you, sir,' Anna replied politely.

'Then play better this time,' the voice commanded.

She played, and she did play a little better, just a little. But then the rustling noise began again, that restless rustling that fatally distracted her as she wondered what it could mean. Was he flipping through her CV trying to find out more about her? Was he following the music, and had she perhaps forgotten a part and he was trying to find his place again? The bow started getting impossibly heavy in her hand again, and she could feel it when she started playing badly. Strangely enough, the rustling noise interfered more with her concentration than the knowledge that she was standing in a state of partial undress on a stage. The noise bothered her more than her awareness of her naked legs, and the embarrassing thought that her pussy must be showing through her tight white panties now that she had lifted the violin up to her shoulder and left her most private part exposed to the penetratingly hot lights as she played.

'I don't think you're quite comfortable enough yet, Miss Li,' the voice abruptly interrupted her piece. 'Do you?'

'Please let me have another chance, sir,' Anna begged. 'I can play better, I really can.'

'This is not really about who can play better, Miss Li. This is about who wants what, and how badly they want it. It doesn't matter so much how well you can play now. Native ability is important, of course, but someone who really wants to learn to play well, someone who *really* wants it, will probably learn to play better than most every one in the long run. And yet no matter how good you are, you cannot get anywhere if you don't have the opportunity. So, in reality, we are not here to find out how well you can play, Miss Li. We are here to find out just how badly you want this award. Just how badly do you want to study the violin?'

'More than anything!' Anna replied passionately.

'Really?' the voice softened, as though her response pleased him. 'Well then, I will let you play that last piece again, but take your panties off first.'

'What?' she gasped.

'You wish to show me how much you want to study the violin, do you not? And you want to be... what was it you said? Oh yes, *comfortable*. Well then, panties down, girl. Now. You cannot possibly be more comfortable than when you're naked and doing what you love best. You are doing what you love best, are you not, Anna?'

'Yes... yes, sir, I am.'

'Well then, strip, and do not make me wait. I am wasting enough time letting you play that last piece again.'

'But...'

'Strip now, or leave. It is your choice, Miss Li. I have another audition inside the hour. We are only running this long because, fortunately for you, you were my last audition before lunch. I am being kind by not sending you straight home. Do you want to be sent home, Miss Li? Or would you prefer that I continue being kind and helpful?'

'I want you to be kind, sir,' she replied softly.

'Then take your panties off, Anna, and let us see what you are made of.'

Anna had to put down her violin. She lay it gently on the stage beside her, propped her bow across its strings, and then straightened up again, her large eyes as strangely blank as a doe's caught in a pair of headlights about to run her over. Then she closed her eyes, and once more tried to pretend she was alone at home as she took hold of both sides of her panties. She had never shown herself to a man before, and she could never have imagined the first time she would do so would be on a stage. But she couldn't let herself think about it, she simply had to take a deep breath, count to three, and do whatever was necessary to get that scholarship. One, two, three... she quickly slipped her panties all the way down her legs, which felt as though they would never end. The lights fell on her small bush, a tuft of jet-black hair thicker and curlier than the hair on her head. She felt his eyes on her - the lights washing over her body were hot with his awareness of her. She squeezed her legs together and put both her hands across her pubic hair to try and hide the lips of her pussy pouting beneath it.

'Do you still want me to play?' she asked sheepishly.

There was a pause, and then she heard movement out in the darkness, the subtle sound of trousers rustling as a man stood up, followed by the sound of slow, unhurried footsteps coming down the aisle towards the stage. He had silver-grey hair, that was the first thing she was able to make out in the darkness just beyond the lights. And then she saw his tall, slender body walking up the steps towards her, completely invisible until that moment because he was wearing a dark suit. Finally, she saw his large and slender hands - a musician's hands.

'I too play the violin, Anna,' was the first thing his embodied voice said to her as he stepped up beside her.

She didn't know quite what to do. In a way, this was worse than standing half naked on a stage beneath anonymous spotlights. This was standing almost completely naked, her pussy shamefully exposed, in front of a strange man... a man with long, knowledgeable fingers...

'Hand me the violin,' he said gently.

Desperately keeping one hand over her mound, she bent over gingerly, and as she picked up the instrument she blushed to realise he was looking at her bare bottom. Too late, she tried to lower her buttocks and crouch down instead of bend over to reach the violin. 'Here,' she said.

'Ah, a Carlson.' He weighed the instrument in his hand. 'Not a bad piece of wood, for the price. But you really should have something better. Would you like something better, Miss Li?'

Now she could see his eyes taking her in, which strangely enough gave his stare even more power over her than when it was just part of the lights. He had arrestingly bright blue eyes the colour of quartz. 'I... I think so,' she replied quietly.

His free hand reached out to touch her with a swiftness that gave her no time to pull back. And he didn't just touch her, he reached into her silk blouse, slipping part of his arm up it like a snake that bit her painfully on the nipple. She squealed just like a mouse, stunned by the abruptness of such an intimate touch. He pinched her nipple, then he spread his hand over her breast and massaged it, taking its measure before cupping it and weigh it gently in his palm. 'Are you quite comfortable now, Anna?' he asked softly, leaning forward slightly so he was almost speaking directly into her ear.

She let herself lean against his dark suit, and closed her eyes. If she didn't look, she didn't have to see that his hand was in her shirt, and she could try not to think about the fact he was pulling on her other nipple now, sending oddly delicious shivers down her spine to her virgin pussy. She had never been touched like this by anyone except herself, and she had never touched herself quite like this...

'Bend over,' he said.

'Pardon?' Anna's eyes opened, but she was surely dreaming.

'You seem a little hard of hearing,' he remarked, 'a dangerous thing for a musician. Assume the position you took just now when you were, very fetchingly, fetching your violin for me. Reach down and touch your toes.'

Even though it made no sense, this was a command Anna could understand, so she bent forward and touched her toes. It put her in a humiliating position, no question about that, and the blood rushed to her head as she realised what part of her he now had every opportunity to inspect leisurely, to his heart's content. And then, to her astonishment, she heard the sound of a violin, not of a violin being played, but of a violin swinging through space. A little jangle rose from its strings as they displaced the air.

'Yes, not a bad instrument, the Carlson, but you really do deserve better if you're going to be my student. Do you want to be my student, Anna? That's what the award pays for, you see, my personal instruction.'

'Oh yes, sir,' Anna whimpered between her knees as she gripped her ankles.

'Good girl,' the judge said. 'Hold still now. Just six strokes should do it, I think.'

'Six strokes?'

'Punishment for attempting to manipulate the judge of a national competition with your attire,' he explained. 'Your bottom needs a bit of an education before you can progress with your training. Hold tight to your ankles.' He swung the violin back down, and smacked her buttocks with it just hard enough for it to seriously hurt, the polished wood making a sharp sound as it connected with her smooth young cheeks. Then he lifted the instrument again, and brought it down a little harder on the bottom half of her delicate rounds, which quivered deliciously beneath the impact. His second blow truly hurt, and seemed to clear her mind as she suddenly realised in disbelief that she was bent over, nearly naked, on the stage of Wigmore Hall with her bum in the air for anyone, and everyone, to see, getting spanked, slowly and methodically with her own violin. And it hurt! Then there was a terrible splintering sound, the unmistakable sound of the delicate box she had played on for the last ten years beginning to give way. The wood, after all, was much less resilient than her soft and yielding bottom. It was the fourth stroke that cracked the instrument. She bit her lip and held on tight, but the fifth blow made her cry out despite herself, and her breathless scream echoed through Wigmore Hall.

'One more,' her judge and future teacher said. 'Be a good girl, or you will not get what is coming to you.'

'Yes, sir.'

The last stroke fell, and the body of the violin broke away from the neck altogether as the box caved in against Anna's buttocks. It fell to the stage with a hopeless clatter, leaving the neck in his hand. He tossed it away as Anna straightened up, putting one protective hand over her pussy again while with the other she caressed the burning cheeks of her bottom. She froze when she saw the great erection thrusting out of his open black trousers like an obscene conductor's wand. His penis was astonishingly white against his dark suit, and she wondered if all cocks were as pale and hard as ivory, except for its head, which was such a lovely purple colour it made her think of a big, juicy grape ready to burst.

'What do I have to do now, sir?' she heard herself ask.

'Do you want to be my student, Anna?'

'Yes, sir,' she answered without hesitation, unable to take her eyes off his magnificent male instrument.

'On your knees then, my girl,' her teacher said.

She sank to her knees, it was easy since they felt so strangely weak, and looked up at his face expectantly.

'Kiss it,' he said. 'You have to learn how to love an instrument before you can handle a good one. Kiss it as you would kiss a beautiful violin.'

She wet her lips with her tongue as she reached out and touched the head of the stiff penis before her with the tip of her finger. It was warm, and tender. She was pleasantly surprised, because his pale shaft had looked so cold and hard. She opened her mouth, which also came naturally since she was already gaping in wonder at the sight before her, and stuck out her pink tongue to give the tip of the judge's prick a tentative little lick. He tasted sweet, like he had bathed in honey-water, and then it just seemed natural to wrap her soft lips around his whole head. She heard him groan above her, and strangely inspired by the sound he made, she rose a little higher on her knees and slipped his whole cock into her mouth.

He fucked her virginal orifice as though it had taken dozens of dicks before, making her moan anxiously as he kept stroking his helmet with the back of her throat and threatening to choke her. Then he pulled out of her abruptly, and even though it was a relief to be able to catch her breath, part of her was inexplicably disappointed.

'Lie on the floor,' he said harshly, 'on your stomach next to your broken violin.'

She did as he told her without question.

He took off his suit jacket, wrapped it around her discarded skirt, and then shoved them both under her tummy. 'Push your bottom up,' he commanded, and she did as he said as he sank to his knees behind her. 'This is your first lesson, Anna.'

She closed her eyes. She couldn't believe it. She would never have dreamed that her first time with a man he would completely ignore her pussy and make her give him her rear hole instead.

'Thrust your bottom back,' he said again, and she did, she thrust her bottom back towards him and let one of his skilled violinist's fingers find her clenched little hole. It felt wet, and she knew he must have licked his finger before he put it in her. Groaning, she found herself thrusting her cheeks back at him as his finger worked between them, making the tight passage between them feel warm and slick, although it was nowhere near as hot and wet as her pussy.

And then his long hard cock entered her. She felt his head pushing against her reluctantly puckered opening, and then he was in. With a hard thrust he breached her sphincter, and his whole shaft slid into her body through her back passage. She groaned in pain and disbelief as he buried his entire erection in her petite bottom, and it felt even worse when he started moving in and out of her, his hips rocking back and forth, back and forth relentlessly. And yet through the initial blaze of torment, she became aware of another sensation brewing in her smouldering pussy. She was lying nearly naked on centre stage in Wigmore Hall, and the idea of what was happening to her, merging with all these new and intense sensations, began to get the better of her... she felt the veins in her body tightening like strings, and she began climaxing under the penetratingly hot lights. She cried out as she came with a strange man's cock pulsing in her rectum, and as she felt him pull his fleshy bow out from between her mysteriously vibrating cheeks, she breathlessly found herself hoping he would let her play for him every night.

The Second Seed

'Lift up your skirt.' The usually smooth old voice sounded harsh and commandingly sharp. Madame Stryker smoothed away a stray lock of white hair that had escaped the severe bun perched on top of her head, accentuating her high cheekbones and broad forehead, as she surveyed the blonde girl standing before her in a short-sleeved white shirt and a crisp pleated tennis skirt.

The girl was Valerie D'Ambois. She was lovely, and she had all the makings of a star. Valeria possessed grace, magnetism and skill, and somehow her gorgeous thirty-six-D breasts did not hinder her movements on the tennis court. Valerie could be a star because people liked looking at her, men in particular, and Madame Stryker, like any truly good coach would, intended to teach Valerie who she was and everything she could be. 'Lift your skirt, girl,' she repeated impatiently. 'I haven't got all day.'

'But...'

'What is it, girl?' the older woman demanded fiercely. 'What have you got to say for yourself?'

'But I won!' Valerie exclaimed, in a soft but nevertheless defiant voice.

'Yes, you won,' her teacher responded just as quietly. 'Of course you won. My pupils *always* win. But *how* did you win?'

'My... my serve,' the blonde girl answered, biting her lip as she realised what was coming.

'Exactly, your serve.' The older woman's voice rose slightly. 'Your serve! And what am I always telling you that you must learn to have?'

'A stride.' Valerie looked down at her tennis shoes.

'A stride to catch the other girl's serve and to bring her down,' Madame

Stryker added, breathing hard now. 'And have you learned that?'

'I'm sorry, madam,' Valerie muttered.

'Lift up your skirt!'

'Not when I've just won.'

'I'll tell you when you've won,' her coach snapped. 'Now show me your bottom.'

Knowing there was nothing else for it, the lovely girl turned around obediently and lifted the short, crisply ironed pleats of her skirt to reveal her perfect pair of cheeks. They were firm but also beautifully full, and right now they were nestled comfortably inside a pair of tight white athletic panties.

'Stick your bottom out,' Madame Stryker commanded.

Valerie complied. She was gritting her teeth, but she complied. At least Madame Stryker had waited until the other girl left before doing this. Valerie knew her teacher enjoyed disciplining students in front of each other 'for the general education of all', as she was wont to say.

'Now bend over, girl.'

Valerie cursed silently, but did as she was told. She had hoped it wouldn't come to this, but the old bat was obviously in a tizzy.

'Down with your panties, and take them off completely. Don't leave them around your ankles. I want you bare.' Madame Stryker spat out her instructions with relish.

Valerie bit her lip again in anticipation, and fear. This was going to be the whole works, and she felt the usual blush warm her face as she reached back, her head more or less parallel with her knees, and pulled down her tight white cotton panties, exposing the taut cheeks of her bottom as she slid them down her slender legs.

Madame Stryker feasted her eyes on the displayed buttocks. They were deliciously round and relaxed, not anxiously clenched; the girl did not yet fear the punishment coming to her. Her blonde bush was just visible above the tender lips of her sex, and also visible was the little rosebud of her anus, which Madame Stryker considered her own personal prize. She knew once she had the girl properly trained that she would perform on the court just as she wanted her to. But Rome was not built in a day, nor was a girl broken in a week. She reached out a hand and rested it lightly against her student's cheeks. 'What have we learned, Valerie?' she asked.

'To be faster on the court?' the girl responded nervously, clinging to her ankles to hold her position.

'We should learn to *obey*,' Madame Stryker said, and lifting her hand, she brought it back down again fiercely across the girl's left buttock.

'Oh!' Valerie cried. 'I'm sorry, madam,' she apologised at once.

'You will pay a penalty,' Madame Stryker decreed, and her hand came down again even harder on the girl's right cheek.

This time Valerie kept quiet, biting her lip from the pain but knowing better than to straighten up and move away. The blows fell one by one, on this cheek, and then that cheek, slowly and regularly, which was how it hurt the most. And then the punishing hand hovered over her blazing cheeks again.

'What have we learned, Valerie?' the severe woman demanded.

'To do as madame says,' Valerie replied meekly and dutifully.

'You have done well, dear girl.' Madame Stryker's fingers slipped between the cheeks of the girl's bottom, and moved down to part the soft and silky lips nestled below.

'Oh...' the girl's mouth fell open, and she moaned as Madame Stryker dipped her fingers into her hot young slot and manipulated her swollen clitoris until she couldn't resist thrusting her hips back against the skilled old hand.

'Do we know how to obey?' Madame Stryker asked quietly.

'Yes, madam, yes,' Valerie sighed, and climaxed as madame flicked her clit swiftly back and forth with a long fingernail. An orgasm making her whole body shudder, she pressed her face against her knees as waves of pleasure crashed through her blood and made her cry out despite herself.

'Today we are playing the full game,' Madame Stryker announced. It was a week later and Valerie was in a tracksuit and running shoes. Beneath the suit she wore a tight vest with no bra, on the insistence of Madame Stryker, who liked to pull the girl's tracksuit bottoms down and get straight to work on the vital matter of proper discipline. 'You have heard me discuss,' Madame Stryker began, 'the difference between the male and the female game.'

Valerie nodded dumbly. She found this was the safest way to respond when madame was in a certain mood, and she was, more often than not, it had to be said, in a certain mood.

'What is the difference between the male and the female game?' madame demanded.

'The masculine game is fuller?' she muttered a guess, unable to remember what her coach had actually said about the two games.

'Stupid girl!' Madame Stryker snapped. She picked up one of the black crops she favoured for private training sessions with her more promising pupils, a hand-stitched leather riding crop with a tightly laced grip at the handle that sat as comfortably in her hand as a conductor's baton. 'What is the difference between the male and female game?' she asked again slowly, her eyes narrowing dangerously.

Thankfully, the answer came swimming out of Valerie's memory. 'Women play the game to be filled,' she replied hastily. 'Men play the game to be emptied.' She smiled, proud of herself.

'Well done,' madame said, just a little sarcastically. 'And do you know what this saying means?'

'Um... no,' Valerie admitted, and now she knew it was going to be one of those days. This time, her relentless coach was really going to give her the works, she could feel it.

'Today, I wanted to show you what the male game is like,' Madame Stryker informed her, 'but I can see that won't be possible. I will have to find another teacher for you, and you can go study with him from now on. What I can teach you will no longer do.'

Valerie's mind reeled from the implication of these words. 'You mean...?'

'Yes,' madame said firmly. 'If what I said has meant nothing to you, if after all this time you haven't a clue what I was trying to tell you, then you had best get yourself a male teacher, and *he* perhaps can show you. I can do no more for you.'

'But madam...' Valerie's voice caught on a sob. She could not believe her esteemed coach and teacher, to whom she was utterly devoted, was just casually dismissing her like this, as though there were no personal feelings between them at all.

'What is it, my girl?' Madame Stryker asked.

'I - I don't want to leave my teacher.' Valerie was appalled to find herself on the verge of tears. She had never felt so upset, not even after losing an important match.

'Then tell me what it means to you to be filled,' madame urged.

Valerie glanced back at her in confusion, tears shining in her lovely, candid eyes. All she could think about was that her teacher was coldly dismissing her. 'What do you mean, madam?'

'You have a boyfriend, don't you?' the older woman demanded. 'His name is Lorain, I believe?'

Valerie's face went crimson with embarrassment. Could she possibly mean...?

'Don't you get filled up by him, Valerie?'

'I... I don't know what you mean, madam,' she replied shyly.

'Do you want me to teach you what I mean, Valerie?'

'P-please, madam.' Anything was better than being sent away by her beloved teacher to continue her training with a complete stranger.

'Then take off your tracksuit bottoms,' Madame Stryker commanded briskly, 'as well as your top and your vest. I want you in just your shoes and socks.'

Valerie began to obey at once.

'You haven't had his cock?' Madame Stryker demanded again as she watched the young woman slip her tracksuit bottoms down her legs, her old eyes on the sweet blonde bush that bloomed into view.

'No, madam.' Valerie's cheeks blushed red as blood oranges, and her pert little nose turned pink beneath her freckles. 'I just let him... I just let him touch me,' she confessed in a barely audible voice.

'He probably contents himself with your beautiful breasts, doesn't he?'

'Yes... but sometimes he... he touches me... down there.' She pulled off her vest and her magnificent bosom sprung into view. Her nipples were erect; she was enjoying being forced to tell madame all her secrets.

'Do you want a male teacher, Valerie?' madame asked the girl who was now standing naked before her except for her tennis shoes and socks, her hands crossed demurely between her thighs.

'I only want you, madam,' she replied, looking into her teacher's hard eyes as her own big blue eyes watered sincerely.

'Then look at this,' madame said, and pointed down ambiguously.

Valerie's eyes followed her teacher's hand, but she could see nothing but the older woman's long black skirt, which bulged a little strangely in the front.

'On your knees, girl,' madame's voice cracked with feeling, 'and you will see what I mean.'

Valerie sank to her knees before the long skirt, which her teacher grasped in both hands and began lifting with the slow drama of a curtain rising in the theatre. And what was revealed was not just madame's legs, which were surprisingly well-honed and firm despite her age, but also something black and shiny that hung down just beneath the hem of the skirt.

'Oh!' the girl breathed. 'What is *that*?'

'Lift my skirt and you will see, my dear.'

Valerie hesitated a moment, and then gingerly reached out and lifted the hem of the skirt up away from the shiny black thing. And then she found herself gazing raptly at her old teacher's still blonde and fragrant pubic hair beneath the tight black leather straps holding the dildo in place. The latex penis was nearly ten inches long and thrust obscenely into the girl's face. 'W-what is it?' she breathed again in awe, scarcely able to believe what she saw.

'It is what will prevent you from having to leave me for a male teacher,' madame replied. 'Open your mouth, my dear.'

'You want me to...?' Valerie's eyes widened incredulously.

'Open your mouth,' madame insisted.

Valerie opened her mouth. The tool was enormous, and tasted, surprisingly, not of rubber but of butter. She realised the smooth black cock-head had been smeared with butter as it breached the barrier of her teeth and kept going, reaching for her throat as madame pushed the long black rubber dick into her mouth.

'Relax your jaw and let it down into your throat, girl. Are you starting to get the idea now what being filled is?'

Valerie's strangled cries responded in the affirmative as madame slowly began fucking her mouth, moving the latex shaft in and out between Valerie's stretched lips as she struggled to breathe. She was beginning to choke when madame finally eased the cool black cock out of her mouth and asked, 'Are you ready to really learn now?'

'Learn what, madame?' She coughed as she swallowed the saliva that had accumulated in the back of her mouth as she swallowed the big rubber cock. And now she realised that sucking on it had made her want something, even though she couldn't say what exactly.

'Go up to my bedroom,' madame ordered, 'and lie on the bed on your front.'

Valerie's eyes grew even wider. 'I never have with Lorain, not with anyone...' she began to protest.

'Do you want a male teacher?' Madame Stryker looked down into the girl's vulnerable eyes with her own steady, unflinching gaze.

'I want to stay with you, madame,' Valerie whispered fervently. 'I'll never want another teacher.'

Madame handed her a tube of cream. 'Go and lie down,' she said again, 'and spread some of this in the tempting valley between your cheeks and over your anus.'

'My... my what?'

'I'll show you what being filled is, Valerie,' madame said gently. 'Come with me upstairs.'

And they went upstairs, hand-in-hand, where Valerie sat down on one side of the bed and opened the small tube of gel while madame stroked her hair. 'Shall I turn round?' the young tennis star asked in a small voice.

'All right,' the older woman said, and pointed to a pillow, upon which the girl rested her cheek so she could push her bottom up into the air as her coach greased the tight space between her cheeks with the cold white lotion. She lay facedown on the bed while her teacher straddled her, and made her stick her bottom out even further, as she had so many times before to be spanked. But this time, Valerie's tautly smooth buttocks met not Madame Stryker's firm hand but something else - the cool black head of the large cock inching its way between her white cheeks, and nudging against the tight little entrance leading to her rear passage.

'Madame...' she whimpered.

'What is it, my dear girl?'

'I love you!' the girl cried passionately, and buried her face in the pillow.

The teacher's face lit up with triumph and her old pussy blazed with the rejuvenating fires of lust as she stroked the girl's hair, and pushed the cruel dildo into her virgin bottom with a short, fierce thrust. Valerie yelped in pain, but her teacher grasped her hair and held firmly onto her head to keep her down. The girl stayed in place as the cock slid in past her opening, and surged all the way down her tight back passage with agonising swiftness. In just seconds, Madame Stryker was inside her, the cruelly long latex erection buried deep between her student's beautiful young buttocks.

'Do you understand what it means to obey?' Madame Stryker whispered, and began sliding the thick black dildo in and out of the girl's deliciously proffered bottom.

'Y-yes, madame,' she gasped. 'To obey is to be filled up...'

'Exactly,' madame answered. 'Do you want Lorain to do this to you?'

'Ooh, um,' she was finding it hard to concentrate on the gentle questions coming from her coach. 'Um, no, madame.'

'Would you prefer a male teacher I select for you, some hairy old oaf, to do this to you?'

She shook her head against the pillow, her cheek buried in its softness, her eyes closed. 'No, madame, I wouldn't.' Valerie bit her lip in agony, and something else... the insistence of the cock was getting to her in a way she could not explain. She was very wet, she realised; her pussy was hot and wet even as she suffered the excruciating impression that the big black dick was ramming itself all the way up into her throat and filling her to bursting.

'Do you want me to tell the other girls that you like this being done to you?' madame asked softly, caressing her hair again.

'Oh no, madam, please don't do that,' Valerie said through gritted teeth, because she was almost there... almost there... the discomfort was constant and yet so strangely sweet... it opened her up and made her feel so tight that the motion of the plastic shaft sliding in and out of her seemed to caress her clit.

'Then who *do* you want to do this to you, my little harlot? Who do you want to fill you up forever?' Madame thrust lustily into the blonde's pert little bottom, her hands gripping the soft and deliciously yielding cheeks.

Valerie whimpered as her coach packed the black cock into her rear, threatening to split her open again and again. 'I'm yours, madame!' she nearly screamed. 'Every part of me is yours. Do with me as you wish. My bottom, everything, is yours. I'm yours, all of me.'

'We'll see, my sweet, we'll see.' Madame laughed softly as she plunged to the very core of the sweet flesh lying beneath her.

Valerie cried out as she came violently, bucking back to meet her teacher's black cock pumping in and out of her bottom, its unnatural length cruelly impaling her on it. Her whole body shook from the force of her orgasm, and she wept breathlessly into the pillow hoping madame would never let her go.

More spanking fun

Bouquet of Bamboo is another scorching collection of spanking short stories, also published by us and available on **AMAZON Kindle**.

Ariadne squealed, reaching back in an effort to cup and protect her scalding cheeks.

'Hands back across the desk, young lady,' the dean ordered sternly. 'No, right across. Further...'

Ariadne's fumbling fingers sought, and found, the desk's far edge. She gripped, swallowing hard as her stomach stretched and her breasts moulded against the unyielding wood, threatening to burst free from her straining bra. At her ankles her stretched panties prevented her from kicking her heels to relieve the pressure.

The dean maintained a meditative silence...

Bamboo is a beautiful wood - more biting than the birch, whippier than the willow wand. So pliant, it spells sharp pain for all punished with the cane. Each searing stroke sounds the serpent's hiss, each crimson weal burns with a fierce bliss. Bamboo bends - as do those doomed for its vicious kiss.

For sullen student and village slut alike, no mercy must be shown - their misdeeds discovered, all must come to the cane. Submitting to the strict discipline dispensed by their stern chastisers, and surrendering to their dominants' dark desires, each must bend over, bare-bottomed, to receive their Bouquet of Bamboo...

www.ingramcontent.com/pod-product-compliance
Lightning Source LLC
Chambersburg PA
CBHW020416130626
46549CB00006B/2589